CRAVE

Catherine Lundoff (signature)

CRAVE

TALES OF LUST, LOVE AND LONGING

CATHERINE LUNDOFF

Lethe
PRESS

ISBN: 1-59021-033-6

Cover art: "A Kiss" by Lorraine Inzalaco, oil on canvas, © 1997
    signed and numbered prints are available from www.inzalaco-lesbianart.com

Interior book design by Toby Johnson

"The Party" appeared previously in *Lip Service* (Alyson Books, 1999).

"Emily Says" appeared previously in *Lust for Life* (Véhicule Press, 2006).

"Hands of a Princess" appeared previously in *Amazons: Sexy Tales of
    Strong Women* (Thunder's Mouth Press, 2006).

"Thursdays at McKinney's" appeared previously in *The Mammoth Book
    of Women's Erotic Fantasies* (Constable and Robinson, 2004).

"By the Winding Mere" appeared previously in *Clean Sheets*, 2000.

The stories are, as always, Jana's fault.

TABLE OF CONTENTS

Spoonbridge and Cherry 9

Kink 18

Leader of the Pack 23

Wage Slave 34

Heart's Thief 44

Blind Faith 57

The Party 65

Emily Says 75

Hands of a Princess 82

Anonymous 94

The Old Spies Club 103

Medusa's Touch 116

Thursdays at McKinney's 135

By the Winding Mere 143

An Evening in Estelí 154

Spoonbridge and Cherry

I'd say that I'd never had sex for money but that would mean forgetting about last winter. But that wasn't about the money, not really. It was about her. Or maybe them. I think.

I was broke, down to my last dime with no job leads on the horizon. It was my own damn fault for a change. I knew the manager at Carol's Coffee was going to fire me and I just didn't bother finding something else to jump to and scrambling for it before the axe fell. Sometimes you gotta play the hand you're dealt. This time I had bad cards and a worse strategy.

It still might have been okay if Michelle hadn't dumped me and kicked me out that same week but they say these things come in threes. I'd say meeting them in the bar few days later was the third one, but then none of it ever would have happened. That would've really sucked, at least looking back on it all now.

That night I was out drinking with my remaining friends, the ones who'd stand you a cheap beer when you were out of work. We were at some dive up in the Northeast, but since it was Minneapolis, none of could ever really say what it was "northeast" of. Not that it mattered.

What did matter was that it was the hellish mid-winter freeze that we get up here, long about February or so. I was killing time before I had to

9

hike the ice-covered blocks back to Kelly's place where I was crashing on the sofa. I was also hoping to find someone to replace Michelle. Which meant I was leaning up against the bar looking as butch and broody as I was capable of in hopes that somebody would buy it.

But the woman who showed up wasn't exactly what I had in mind. For one thing she was older, like old enough to be my grandma kind of old. For another, she didn't look right. Even in the flickering neon, her blues eyes had that junkie stare going on, the kind where they look right through you and never blink. She was dressed nice though. Good watch, good shoes so she must've had some cash, at least before she got hooked on whatever it was.

Just then those eyes were fixed on me and I was trying not to back away. Finally she said, "Hello," in the most normal voice in the world. I nodded, then turned back to watch the pool game while the space between my shoulders got all prickly. She kept talking like she knew I wasn't ignoring her. "I'm looking for someone to do something for me. Something I'm willing to pay for. And I overheard you saying that you were out of work."

I whipped around to stare down at her, my mood bouncing between seriously creeped out and crazy pissed off. She smiled then, a thin-lipped, twisted scary smile that didn't make anything look any better to me. Pissed off won. "I don't know who the hell you think you are--"

"My apologies. I'm a rude old woman and I don't have much time left. Not enough to play social games anyway. So for your information, you were whining about being broke and getting fired and dumped loud enough for them to hear you down at the Mall of America." She gave me a once-over and I finally saw her blink. Except now she looked like I wasn't worth her time.

I opened my mouth to snarl something back at her and what came out was "Yeah, so what? Not like it's any of your business. Whyncha' just leave me alone to get drunk in peace?" I turned to walk away and she grabbed my arm. Not tight, but just enough to slow me down from storming off.

When I stopped, she let go. "It's about her. That's why it's my business." She nodded over at a table in the corner. "Normally, I could care less. But now…well, you look a bit like me when I was younger, back before I got sick. I think that might make her happy. And that's all that matters to me right now." I followed her nod over to the table.

There were three old dykes sitting around it drinking their beers and trading war stories. I ignored them. But the fourth one, she made my heart stop. I used to think that was pure b.s. but man, was I wrong. She had blonde hair and blue eyes, standard Nordic goddess for these parts. Except that she was the most beautiful woman I'd ever seen. She smiled and the rest of the room went away, even though she wasn't smiling at me. No, that smile was being thrown away on the scary old junkie standing next to me. There is no justice in this world.

The scary junkie smiled back and I started to change my opinion. Maybe she wasn't hopped up after all. Sometimes they kept the stare up for years after they went clean. Whatever. Not my problem. For a minute, I considered making a play for the blonde, the notion sending a hot wave up my thighs.

"So I take it you're interested?" Those weird blue eyes were fixed on me again. "It's a worth a couple of hundred if you're in."

"Wha—say, what is your deal? You looking for a third or something?" For a moment, I seriously considered it. Beauty and the Beast. Yeah, that'd be one to share with my buddies, probably worth a couple of beers. I imagined the blonde minus that bulky sweater, her sweet curves under my expert hands. I started getting wet, forgetting for the moment that there'd be a third party participating. The crazy woman inched closer and my little fantasy went up in smoke. No way. Not even for the goddess.

"Not what you've got in mind?" She gave me a wicked smile, one that made me madder and hotter all at the same time.

"I can handle anything you can dish out." I growled the words, wishing a moment later that I hadn't. This one could be into just about anything. But it was too late now and I was too down and out to take it back.

"Good. Let's go before you chicken out." And she turned and walked away, not bothering to look back to see if I was following her.

I wasn't. I leaned against the bar and watched her walk over to the blonde, saw the blonde smile up at her again, and winced. Then the blonde looked at me and I had to catch my breath. She didn't look too thrilled as far as I could tell. But maybe she frowned like that every time her crazy girlfriend picked up a third. I pulled myself together and gave her my best cool smile, the one that says that I'm every girl's dream, especially at bar closing time.

The maniac with her waved me over and I sauntered across the room, my eyes never leaving the blonde's. "Hi. I'm—"

But the nut job cut me off. "We don't need to know. And you don't need to know ours. It's not important for what I've got in mind."

I glared at her but she wasn't paying attention. Instead the blonde shrugged, then got up to help the other one into her jacket. From the way she was looking at the old bat, it was obvious they'd been together for awhile. *Why?!* A little voice wailed in the back of my head. I told it to shut up and followed them out, ignoring the whispers behind me. Maybe they did this every week. Who knew?

The other two led the way to a small SUV in the parking lot. I think it was green but I couldn't be sure. I didn't bother to get the plates either, stupid me, not that I cared until later. Then we were off, headed across town. Crazy woman cut me off every time I tried to talk so after a few tries, I just sat in the back and looked at the blonde's profile. You could tell she had her doubts about whatever her partner had planned but she was going along with it anyway.

For the life of me, I couldn't figure out why. The other one just seemed like a nut to me, and a sick nut to boot. I wondered what was wrong with her and guessed the Big C, just because. Not like I could ask anyway. Then I tried to picture myself in bed with them. That helped, for some weird reason. At least it helped when I saw myself going down on the goddess and burying my face in her sweet pussy.

I could almost feel her start to come when we got to Loring Park. Then Crazy Eyes slowed down like she was going to stop. Then it hit me: she was figuring on some kind of outdoor scene. I started to panic. A couple of hundred bucks wouldn't help me if I died from exposure. The SUV followed the curve around the park while I looked for a way to turn down whatever they had planned. By the time I'd gotten to "Thanks, but no thanks," she'd crossed the street and parked up past the Walker and the Sculpture Garden.

"So…we're headed back to your place, right? Wherever that is?"

They ignored me in favor of their own conversation. "You sure you want to go through with this?" The blonde asked.

"Long as you're okay with it, love. You know I've wanted to bring you back here to do this for a long time. This looks like it's as close as we're going to get." Then they stared at each other forever and smooched like I wasn't there.

"Ummm…hello? When do I get a piece of the action?" I was getting tired of being ignored and pissed off was better than nothing.

Blondie broke off the kiss and turned around at that. She reached out and pulled me forward so my face was right in front of hers. She stared at me for so long I lost some feeling in my toes. Then she kissed me. Hard. My lips opened under her tongue and I kissed her back with everything I had. Didn't even hear the other one get out of the truck.

When we stopped for air, I had to ask, "So where'd she go?"

"She had something to take care of. Don't worry about it." The goddess was a woman of few words, just the way I liked them. I smiled as she kissed me again. The touch of her lips was sending a hot wave of pure lust through everything from my ribcage on down. I wondered if she was getting half as wet as I was and if I could stick my hand between her legs to find out.

Crazy Eyes came back right about then. "We're all set. You ready?" This was to her girlfriend of course; guess I always looked ready or something.

"You sure?" The goddess asked like she already knew the answer to that question.

Crazy Eyes jerked her head in a nod, then pulled my door open. "Let's go." I got out, moving kinda slow like I thought I could delay whatever they had in mind. But I was aching for the blonde, all hot and empty until I knew I wouldn't say no to anything that wasn't really scary. The goddess grabbed my arm and started towing me back down the hill toward the museum and the Sculpture Garden.

We went down the hill past the condos and mansions and our breath was a frozen white cloud around us, which probably meant I was panting. Downtown was crystal clear in the frigid air, all the little lights on the skyscrapers twinkling their hearts out. The snow cover was just right, fresh and white and sparkling in front of us as we got to the greenhouse with its big glass fish.

They'd found a way into the greenhouse after hours? That must be it. Well, I figured that'd be okay, or warm at least. But the goddess kept going, pulling me along in her wake. What the hell did she have in mind? Lights went off all over the snow as we hit the motion detectors' sensors and I blinked at the statues and stuff. I hoped to hell the place wasn't alarmed too or we'd be meeting Minneapolis' finest pretty soon.

I was making noises about hotels and the SUV and common sense when I looked up and realized what she was headed for. Oh shit. The sculpture of the bigass metal spoon with the cherry on top. Probably the only thing the rest of the country recognized about Minneapolis and we were just going to wander up and do what? Take nekkid pictures in front of it until my tits dropped off from the cold?

"Spoonbridge and Cherry," the goddess murmured, like saying the thing's name out loud made the whole thing make more sense.

I was still sputtering when I noticed Crazy Eyes walking over to sit down on one of the benches. She was holding herself like she was in pain or something. The goddess let go of me and started over to her but stopped when she shook her head. I decided the time had come to take off, gorgeous woman or no gorgeous woman. But the goddess turned out to be in better shape than me and I went down on my face in the snow when she tackled me.

Nothing like a snoot full of snow to get a girl in the mood. I twisted around so I was face up and tried to flip the blonde over. She locked her legs around one of mine and moved to pin my arms down. I twisted my hand loose and grabbed one of her arms and that was about the time I noticed that her perfect face was an inch away from mine. Her lips were set in a line and she was frowning so I kissed her.

This time, I took her by surprise and was able to flip her onto her back in the snow. She opened her legs and wrapped them around my waist so I decided to stay put for a few minutes. Her lips were icy on mine but it was warm, no hot, inside her mouth. Her tongue shoved its way past my teeth and I sucked on it, wrestling it with mine.

Once I was distracted, she raised her hips up and twisted out from under me. Next thing I knew, she had me by the collar and was dragging me through the snow toward that damned sculpture. I grabbed some snow, then some frozen grass under it but I only managed to get my gloveless hands wet and cold. I had a fuzzy memory of there being water under the spoon that being what made it a 'bridge,' but it was my lucky night and Hell had frozen over.

I slipped and slid along behind her until we got right up to the stupid thing. But no lights or alarms went off. I finally realized that they had a buddy in the Walker, which meant someone else was watching our little production. I wasn't sure if I felt better or worse about that. The blonde snapped snow-covered fingers in front of my nose. "Hey, wake up. Remember me? Climb on up here, tiger and show me what you've got. We have a show to put on."

I stared at her as she climbed up into the spoon just below the cherry. She stared back at me, her expression shifting from Norse love goddess to Valkyrie. I followed her up into the thing, shivering the whole time. Nothing says fun like balancing in a giant metal spoon in the middle of a Minnesota winter. The blonde took a deep breath and grabbed my hand. Then she shoved it up under her coat and sweater, up to where the nipples in her big soft breasts were trying to turn themselves to stone under my frozen fingers.

That did it. I pulled her close, my tongue wrapped in hers and my hands getting warmer by the second. I imagined what she looked like without eighteen layers of clothes, maybe in a nice soft bed. Indoors. But I needed to work with what I had. I broke away from the kiss and dropped to my knees in front of her so I could suck on her hard little nipples.

The goddess moaned deep in her throat, possibly from impending frostbite and I slipped a hand between her legs and started rubbing through her pants and all. I decided not to think about the woman on the bench and whoever else was watching through the security cameras. Or at maybe I just decided it was hotter this way, playing to an audience. I tongued one icy nipple against my teeth and she yanked my hat off and buried her fingers in my hair.

I could feel the crotch of my jeans getting damper but I couldn't spare a hand to get between my own legs, not the way the goddess was gasping for air now. Instead, I concentrated on standing up and getting my thigh between hers. I started unsnapping her pants as I kissed her, licking my way over her ear and neck. She bit me then, sinking her teeth into my earlobe until I yelped. Her icy fingers were under my jacket and sweater now, working their way up. I was mumbling some b.s. about how hot she was as I got my own hand down into her hot moist fur and her soaking wet slit.

She sucked my earlobe harder and groaned into my ear, almost a growl. I shoved my leg against her, driving a couple of my fingers into her pussy. She got even wetter and I kept going, setting up a rhythm that was getting both of us warmed up more by the second. I could tell she was getting close from the way she was breathing and it made me grin.

From the corner of my eye, I saw her girlfriend make some movement that looked like she was getting happy in her own pants. Always good to know your work is appreciated. I bared my teeth and bit the goddess' neck, working on one of those huge high school type hickeys that no turtleneck will ever completely cover up. Normally I'm classier than that but I wanted to mark her, make her mine even for a little while. Her pussy walls closed on my fingers then and she wailed into the frozen air, legs shaking around mine as she came.

She grabbed my face and kissed me again, eyes closed and I guessed that she was imagining being there with the girlfriend. To hell with that. I shoved her hand down my pants, startling her enough that her eyes shot open. If she was hot before, she was smoking now: big blue eyes all cloudy from sex, white teeth chewing on pink lips. She found my clit so fast I thought it must be about 3 feet long by now, then she flipped me around so I was in the spoon.

Her hand forced my legs apart so she could get just about all her fingers inside me. I was plenty warm enough now, even when she yanked up my sweater and bit my tit. Then she pulled some snow from the cherry and rubbed it into my nipple. She warmed my nipple back up with her mouth, then she did it again until I thought I'd pass out from being roasting hot then freezing cold.

All the while her fingers were rubbing and pinching my clit until I couldn't take it anymore. I came hard, with only her hand inside me still holding me up, I was shaking so hard. Some lights flickered on in one of the condos nearby and I realized I'd been making a hell of a lot of noise.

That was when Crazy Eyes showed up next to us, making me jump. "Time to go," she growled. The goddess didn't argue, just zipped up her pants and tapped me on the cheek and jumped down. Her girlfriend stuffed a couple of bills in my pocket and the next thing I knew, I was standing around freezing my ass off watching them walk away. I zipped up my pants and pulled my shirt down, shivering now from being completely frozen. I followed them out but when I got to the street, they were nowhere to be seen and there was a cab idling in front of the museum.

I looked around, hoping for one last glimpse but my bad luck still held. Figuring the cab was for me, I hopped in and headed back to Kelly's. Everything was all sticky and achy and even the crinkle of new bills in my pocket didn't make it all better. I wanted the goddess for my very own and it wasn't to happen and that depressed the hell out of me. Even getting a job a few days later didn't help that much, at least not at first. The blonde was the only thing I saw when I closed my eyes. Plus I couldn't figure out whether it was hotter that I got paid for the best sex I've ever had or not.

But eventually I stopped looking for them in the local dives and got myself a new girlfriend. Blonde hair, blue eyes, standard Nordic goddess for these parts. Maybe someday soon, I'll take her by the Sculpture Garden and see how she likes art.

KINK

It began with small things. Carol realized that later. At the time, they seemed insignificant, little things of no importance. She was pretty sure it started with the smell, that warm scent that leather gets when it's well cleaned. And well used. The second part took longer to notice, of course. But once she recognized it, it was impossible to ignore.

Then there was the touch, the feel of it against her skin. When she wore the right outfit, the perfect leather shoes, she was a sex goddess, a woman no one could ignore. She stood straighter and taller, stepped out more confidently, skin and pussy tingling as if on fire. She met the glances, jealous or admiring, that came her way. And she soaked her panties thinking about all the things she could do with her admirers until her thighs were slick.

It started with the shoes: gorgeous high-heeled ones with pointed toes and razor-thin heels. There was something irresistible about them, that first pair that she bought after a bad day. She was walking home, her sensible shoes making her feel dowdy and hopeless, when she saw them. Moments later, they were hers, though afterwards she couldn't remember even trying them on.

They made her feel wonderful, even if she couldn't keep them on for very long. That wasn't really the point, was it? If they provided the opportunity to slip them off and let her run her bare feet up her lover's bare calves, that was enough. It was enough to see the look on his face when he picked her up for a date and looked at her feet. Almost enough, anyway.

After the shoes, came the boots: full-length black leather ones that ran up her thighs. She loved slipping her calves into the warm softness of the leather. Loved caressing her legs and watching herself in the mirror.

Soon, the boots were the only thing she wore when she got home. She rubbed them all over her naked body once the door was safely locked behind her. She slid them between her legs until her clit burned from the pressure and the leather got warm and hot and wet from her desire.

Then she would slip her fingers inside them and rub herself to orgasm, using sometimes the toe, sometimes the calf. She would pause to watch her own face in the mirror on the back of her bedroom door. To run a hand over her breasts and ribs like a caressing hand or tongue until she shook with the power of her not quite sated longings.

Her lover knew about this, of course. He liked to watch her do things to herself with the boots, liked to watch her parade around in nothing but thigh-high black leather boots with spiked heels. But he always wanted more. Eventually, he wanted her to put the boots away and embrace his flesh the same way she touched her own and watch him in the mirror the way she watched herself.

But it wasn't the same. He never got to see that look of wild abandon that she wore when it was just her and the boots and the mirror. So he went away, leaving her alone. That was when she realized the boots might not be enough.

She found the leather vest at a second-hand shop on her way home from work one night. It looked like it had belonged to a biker once; she could still see the old Harley logo on the back. It laced up the sides and it was worn thin and soft. It was a little tight on her when she buttoned it closed but she thought she might get to like that. She buried her face in it, breathing deep until she ached so badly it was all she could do not to rub herself off in the store's little changing room.

When she got back to her apartment, she yanked off her office clothes as if they were on fire. Then she put her boots on and stood in front of her mirror. She slid the vest over her bare breasts, shivering with delight at the touch of the velvety leather. Then she took it off and ran it up her thighs. Then worked a corner of it into her pussy, twisting it so it rubbed her clit. After that she put it back on, buttoning it so that it pushed her breasts up at the top.

She looked at her reflection wearing nothing but thigh-high leather boots and the biker vest. Her fingers found her clit, then her pussy, then finally her asshole, all hot and aching to be filled and touched all at once. When she came, she had to brace one hand against the wall so that she didn't fall over.

Then she went to her big soft bed and rubbed herself off on an old boot, imagining that the biker who had worn the vest was there with her. Imagining the feel of other hands on her nearly naked body, another's leather-covered body rubbing against her as her fantasy lover took her hard in an orgy of bewitching scents.

But there was still something missing.

She got up and went into the bathroom. She pulled out her razor and shaving cream and she shaved her pussy down to the bare soft skin. She touched the vest to the delicate flesh and nearly shrieked at the shock that went through her. It made her smile.

More importantly, it made her shop. She combed through every store in the city until she found the perfect black leather skirt, the perfect red leather corset. She wore nothing under them when she walked around the apartment, savoring the feel of her new wardrobe against her bare skin. She found a dildo and covered it with leather strips. When she fastened it to her bedpost then backed up to it, engulfing it with her flesh, she could imagine she was being taken by a lover who wore nothing but leather. The image filled her dreams.

She began wearing leather skirts and higher heels to work. Once she even found a pair of Italian leather heels with chains that hung from the ankle straps so that their delicate weight caressed her feet. She imagined wearing them with her leather corset, imagined walking into a bar and having everyone there want her.

After that it was just a matter of finding the right bar.

She looked around until she found the city's one leather bar, where she was lucky enough to be adopted by some of the Bears. They thought she was cute and even called her "Goldilocks" because it made her giggle. They told her wonderful things about custom-made chaps and harnesses and the things you could do when you wore them.

Most importantly, they introduced her to Michelle. Michelle had a bike of her own and wore chaps and a braided quirt at her belt. She even wore fine black leather gloves, encasing hands that fascinated Carol. When she wore her vest, it fastened with thin silver chains that ran across her breasts, coaxing her nipples into near permanent hardness beneath her black t-shirt. More than anything, Carol wanted to take those nipples into her mouth and suck them. She wanted to ride Michelle's bike and press her naked shaved pussy into Michele's chaps while the engine throbbed into her through the leather seat.

At first, she was a little surprised, even shocked, by her fantasies. But not for long. Michelle smelled like leather, well cleaned and well used, even when she wore office drag. Whenever she met Carol for lunch, she always managed to get close enough to touch her. She held Carol's leather jacket for her, she brushed her hand against her leather-covered hip as if by accident, she mentioned the new chaps she was getting that weekend.

But she didn't do any more than that and it was nowhere near enough for Carol. So when she couldn't take it any more, she invited Michelle to the bar. Then, concealed by the table, she spread her legs as wide as they would go in the tight sheath skirt she was wearing. She took Michelle's gloved hand and guided it into her waiting, aching self.

They left the bar soon after that.

When they got to Michelle's bike, she unzipped Carol's skirt enough so that Carol could ride behind her on the seat. Enough so that she could feel Carol's shaved pussy with her gloved fingers. Carol noticed that she didn't take her gloves off and that made Carol very happy.

Once Carol was sitting on the bike, rubbing the leather seat with her bare, wet skin, Michelle kissed her and it was everything that

Carol had been dreaming about. When she got on and started the bike up, Carol thought she might come from the vibration alone.

But she was afraid of falling. Instead, she clung on with her hands and legs and pressed herself as close to Michelle as she could get. Everything she could touch and everything she could smell was leather and she was empty and aching and wet when they got to her apartment. As they went up the stairs, Michelle touched her with her gloved fingers, touched her in all the places that begged to be filled, until Carol was all hers. Almost.

When they got into her apartment, Michelle saw the high-heeled boots and the leather vest and she pulled off the skirt that Carol was wearing. Then she made her kick off her heels and take off her corset. After that, Carol put on the vest and the boots and stood in front of Michelle in nothing but those, her pink and bare-naked pussy inches from Michelle's lips. Michelle explored her with her tongue and Carol thought it was much better than the mirror.

Michelle pulled her into the bedroom and Carol showed her the leather dildo. Then Michelle made her lie on the floor in front of the mirror while she licked her clean-shaven pussy and fucked her with one black-gloved fist. And Carol bucked and moaned and wailed and watched herself in the mirror.

Then Michelle took the leather dildo and she worked it up Carol's ass. She stuck three gloved fingers inside Carol and sucked her clit. Carol burst the buttons on the old vest when she came. She even stopped looking in the mirror. That made Michelle smile.

Michelle let Carol bury her face between her own leather-covered thighs. She let Carol drive her fingers inside her and play with herself at the same time until they both came. Michelle smiled at their reflection in the mirror as she ran her gloved hands over Carol's naked skin. And this time it was enough and more than enough and they even smiled at each other.

Leader of the Pack

Snow crunches beneath the pack's paws as we race behind you. The cold runs through my own paws and up my legs until I shiver in spite of my thick coat. The moon breaks free from the clouds, lighting our way and you greet it with a howl that makes me want to roll over, throat exposed. Giving myself to you.

I surrender to the wolf and I howl with you. The pack joins us, sending our voices high into the trees. From far away, I smell prey on the wind and I suck in the scent eagerly, drawing it down my muzzle like a drink of fresh water. I pause and now you smell it too. You turn, circling me, tongue lolling from your jaws in a doggy grin. I imagine its touch on my human parts for a moment and whine eagerly, hopefully.

Instead, you turn, racing away toward the bewitching smell and I run after you, the rest of the pack at my heels. Now all I breathe in is the musky scent of you, my alpha, my queen. With the part of me that is not-wolf, I wonder what I breathe when I can't smell you. Then the wind shifts and everything is blood and the hunt and I push desire away. I become wolf, closing the door on my human self, letting it dream of you.

When next that self wakes, I taste blood and there is blood on the snow all around me. A crumpled body of some sort lies at the edge of the clearing and I make myself see it only with wolf eyes. It was prey and then it was food. Nothing more. I do not look at it again.

Instead I roll in the snow, cleansing my fur of whatever it is that I have eaten. Around me the pack dozes but you are awake. I walk silently to your side and whine a question. You point upward with your snout and I follow your movement in time to see the moon slide toward the horizon. Then you turn and walk out of the clearing, leaving me to trail after you as we make our way back to our human selves. Spell broken, none of the others follow us this time.

We walk toward danger, toward the scent of humans and I wander after you as if there is no other way. As if we have never spoken of staying wolf. There are sharp smells, alien things, not like the snow or the wind. I whimper as I change back, whine as my bare human feet touch the icy coldness of the snow. Without my fur and fangs, without my pack, I am weak and the cold can kill me. I struggle not to expose my human throat, to roll on my back and surrender to it.

My human self seizes control as the moon sets and I race for the pile of clothes and blankets we left at the edge of the woods. You tackle me so that we fall on the soft fabric, your naked body pressed against mine. My feet are buried in snow and I flail, bucking against you. I feel your muzzle shorten to a human jaw against my neck, your teeth nip my flesh. You hold my hands above my head with one sinewy arm while your hand plows into me without preamble, knowing I am always ready for you. I howl at the shock of cold human fingers inside me and strain against them, riding them until my back arches and I shiver and shake with release.

You look down at me, your expression an echo of the wolf's smile, and release my arms. I sink on my knees in the snow before you, trying to will my shivers away, and I bury my face between your legs. You delight in my homage, in my discomfort almost as much as the sensation of my tongue on your flesh. You are alpha in truth and I am never allowed to forget my place in the pack.

The knowledge makes me send my hand between your legs as my thighs run wet and hot with my own longings. I am yours and the thought makes me grin my own version of your doggy smile. I lick harder, using my fingers to probe your secret places. You growl, the last of the wolf leaving with the moon and embrace my whole hand, pulling it inside you until I think I will never get it back. The notion thrills me and I press harder until you come around my clenched fist and wail your release into the winter air.

Then I feel the cold around me, the frozen places on my bare flesh and I pull a blanket from the pile. You might have let me have it before but that would not have been enough for you. You are always testing me even when I sleep in your arms and dream of nothing but you. Your lips touch mine fiercely and I open to you until you pull away to get dressed. I fight the urge to hold on, knowing it won't do me any good.

We are human inside and out now, at least until the next full moon. Then wolf again next month and on and on until we meet the silver bullet of legend or fail from disease or old age. I glance behind me at the trees and pull in the scents of pine, of freedom. Then I turn and reluctantly follow you back to the world where you are the town sheriff and I am nothing more than the waitress at the local café. Not even your beta. I bite back a whimper.

Each time, it's a little harder to turn back. We've all heard the stories of the ones who went wild, surrendering their human selves to live in the woods. All the other were in the chatrooms claim to know someone who's "gone wolf" but since they never come back, no one knows for sure. Right now, I want that. I want to belong to you, to be possessed by you casually and fiercely, surrendering myself to pack law.

But you have power as a human and you will not let it go. This I know as I watch you fasten your belt and check your gun in its holster. You are the woman who became sheriff against the odds and you can no more deliberately lose that battle than you can cease to be alpha. You grin at me then as though you can read my thoughts.

As we walk back on the trail, I see something from the corner of my eye and I turn to meet the eyes of the man who stands there, watching us. "Sheriff, Kim." Pete Lassiter nods at us. Instinctively I bristle. He was your rival when you ran for sheriff, saying as often as he could that no woman could keep the town safe.

Tonight he has a rifle over his shoulder and wears camouflage. "Cold night for hiking, ain't it?" He raises one bushy eyebrow and as I stare into his blue eyes, I realize he suspects that I belong to you. But his expression does not change and he is not a direct threat. I force the ghost of my hackles down.

"Kim here thought she saw some poachers back in the woods. Thought we'd see if there was anything going on before we called the rangers in." Your fingers find the butt of your gun unconsciously, daring him to ask if the woods aren't too dangerous for two women alone at night.

He doesn't ask. Instead he says the thing I fear most to hear from a human with a rifle. "Thought I heard wolves. Haven't had a pack in these woods in years but I figured I'd go have a look. Maybe bag me a coyote if nothing else."

My wolf-self howls inside me. The pack is all and I must protect them, must stop this man with his bullets. I hear the breath hiss through your teeth as you fight a little for control. "Wolves ain't for shooting, Pete. You know that. 'Less you got some cows or poultry you're protecting that I don't know about?" Your voice is calm, just one more guy among guys. No unspoken threat hums beneath your words and despite myself, I relax.

Lassiter nods agreement. "Just carrying this for my own protection, Sheriff. Got no intention to go hunting. I know the law." And with that, he nods at me and crunches off into the snow, headed back toward the sleeping pack. I watch your face as he goes and I see your lip curl, exposing a white tooth. For an instant, your face is longer and your eyes are golden and I tremble for us both.

But the moment passes and we do not follow him; they will smell him before he gets there and do not need our help. Instead we walk silently back into town and go our separate ways. I remember the taste of you on my tongue for as long as I can. Then I go to the diner and pour coffee and serve eggs as if none of it ever happened. I nod to you when you come in with your men. I joke and flirt with them, knowing that it means nothing.

I cannot do the same with you and my knees shake whenever you look my way. Even here you are the center of attention and your men follow you like a human pack, instinctively recognizing a true alpha. You do not bluster or brag but we all know that you will kill to defend us, that you may done so already. Our town has had no meth labs, no serious crime since you became sheriff, not like the towns around us. Rightly or wrongly, we believe that it is because of you.

Here in my space, you are just another dark-haired woman with amber eyes turning golden in the right light. I try not to think about how much I want to see them change. You have a career and shared custody of your children to consider. Your ex would never let them be raised by a lesbian, let alone a werewolf. You might even lose the next election, though I doubt that more than you do. But for your sake, I make myself look away and think about something else.

I know I will not get closer to you than this until we are wolf again. I know that this is the one time that you fear me, fear what I might cost you if the town knew. But I love you too much to ask you to pay the price of being with me, of acknowledging what we are. Instead, I dream of you and haunt the were chatrooms until the moon fills my blood again.

This time, you take me as we change, your face lengthening and your hands turning to paws as you grind yourself against me. My own hands paw at the snow beneath them as I scramble for purchase, for release. Your fur mingles with mine as it sprouts and I let you rest your wolf-fangs against my still human throat as I embrace you. I thrill to the danger, remembering how you made me were, seducing me with my own longings for freedom until I could not refuse you. My whines fill the night as I surrender to the heat of desire.

Then you are all wolf and I change to follow you, to run behind you as we search for the pack. For the first time, I wonder how many of them are were. They are larger than normal wolves, and smarter too. None of them seems to fall victim to traps or to the death sentence of raiding the local farms. Surely there is something more than your once-a-month leadership that keeps them safe. Once again, I vow to be there when they change back, if they do. Once again, I know I will do what you do and leave when you leave.

The temporary alpha snarls a little when we appear but he meets your eyes and yields. I grin a lolling doggy grin where he cannot see me. It is right that you should be alpha. I can imagine you no other way. One of the others gives me an almost human wink but her face shifts and I cannot be sure.

I scratch at the snow, wanting to be off and running for the joy of it but we must obey the pack protocols. You establish your dominance quietly and none of the others try to fight you for it, even though you are a female. Then and only then do you turn to run from the clearing, knowing we will follow you through anything.

But something is wrong tonight. The air doesn't smell right and there are men in the woods, men who smell of metal and fear. We run further than we have ever run before, hoping to leave them far behind us. A deer leaps out in front of us, running further into the wild. Together we race after her, our howls muted at your growl.

At your heels, we dart over rocks and through an icy stream, confusing the tracks behind us. You lead us up the mountain and finally, the scent of men falls away behind us. Now we are free to hunt and feast on whatever we can catch and you yip playfully as we flush a rabbit, then two. The others find more prey and we feast on the warm bodies and look out over the valley at the lights of town far below us.

I sit near you, the shreds of my human self imagining a different future as I look from the lights to you. You turn and nip gently at my shoulder, acknowledging my gaze. Then you lead us further up the mountain, running as fast as you can and leaving us to catch up. You howl very softly when we reach the top, stretching your neck upward to the moon. We look for permission to add our voices to yours but it does not come.

You think we are still in danger; I see this through both wolf and human eyes and I bow to your judgment. We follow you down the far side of the mountain, until the moon begins to sink. You lead the pack to some caves, out of sight of the lights of town and we leave them there. I follow you back in a slow and careful circle through the same woods we ran through freely last month. My wolf self aches to run, free and wild through the snow, just as my human self aches for your fears for our safety.

We hid our clothes out of sight this time, away from where we met Lassiter. The woods reek of men and guns and I nearly whimper as we slide past them through the trees like shadows. Pete Lassiter stands between us and our hiding place and I watch the moon sink with horrified eyes, knowing that there is no choice between being a naked woman in the winter woods and a wolf surrounded by armed men.

But our luck stays with us and he moves on, snow crunching beneath his feet. We slink into the hollow surrounded by bushes just as we begin to change. You give me an unreadable golden stare and I tremble with want in spite of the danger. I can see you smell my desire, see yours rise with mine but still you make no move, choosing to get dressed instead. I meet your eyes, holding them with mine as I tug on my shirt and socks.

I pull my pants on but leave them unzipped as I send my hand into the aching wetness between my legs. You watch me, eyes growing human dark with desire as I caress my flesh, chewing my lip to keep myself quiet. I imagine that it is your hand, your tongue on me and I close my eyes so I can forget about the cold, the danger. The way that you shiver while you watch me but refuse to touch me.

A crunch of footsteps on snow brings me back to myself and I yank my hand from between my legs. You tense as if to spring and I see your gun glint in your hand, one of the few times I have ever seen you draw it. I hold my breath, waiting for what comes next. The footsteps circle our hiding place, pause, then move on. But your gun stays in your hand as you crouch, waiting and listening.

I lace my boots on as silently as I can and zip up my pants. I do not meet your eyes this time. I can't. I should never endanger the pack alpha like I have tonight, not now when we are hunted. I ache with shame, with unfulfilled longings as you finish getting dressed. You go ahead of me, waving me forward as you stop at each shadow. Your gun stays in your hand and I shiver whenever the fading moonlight falls on it.

It seems like forever but we finally reach the safety of the edge of town without the hunters seeing us. I slink away from you, my head bowed as I walk away. For the first time, I realize that I will have to leave, to move far from you. One werewolf in town can be invisible. Two stand out. I remember Lassiter's eyes and I wonder how many others suspect, how many others watch my eyes follow you. I can only bring you danger of one kind or another.

I'm almost home when I hear footsteps behind me. I pull my keys from my pocket, working them between my fingers the way you showed me. With my other hand, I pull my cell phone from my pocket, letting the streetlights glint off it as I turn. You are on me so fast that I almost slash you with the keys before I realize that it's you. Your body presses against mine, driving me backward into the darkened alley next to my apartment building.

Your mouth is hot on mine in the dark of the basement doorway and I shove the keys and the cell phone away so I can hold you. I pull you closer with fearful longing, terrified that this may be the last time I get to feel you against me like this. You thrust your leg between mine until my clit catches fire through my jeans and I gasp for air against the skin of your throat. With a single gesture, you touch your finger to my lips and I am silent, obeying your commands.

You slide a cold hand up my shirt, caressing and pinching my nipples into diamond-hard points. You run your tongue down my neck, then bite my throat. I arch my head back, yielding to your mouth, your teeth, your hands. And you take what I have to give, your hand finding its way inside my jeans, your fingers shoved hard inside me, filling the aching want you find there.

I ride your fingers, gasping for air in the winter dawn, grasping at your scent, your taste. Drowning myself in you. I can feel your desire as I stagger and sway in your arms. When my knees are stable again, I drop to them in front of you, burying my face in your jeans. They are damp against my mouth and I feel a shudder run through you as I unzip your fly. I wedge my tongue inside, thrusting it through the soft wetness of your fur. For a fleeting moment, I wonder if your eyes are golden. Then I lose myself in you, lose myself bringing you whatever ecstasy I can.

When I am done, when you have stopped shaking against my body, I remain kneeling, my face pressed into your thigh. "I'm so sorry." I murmur against the denim of your jeans. "I never should have done that."

You don't ask what "that" I mean but I feel you laugh a little. "Well your timing could have been better. Just don't do it again or it might get us into trouble." You tilt my face up so you can see my eyes. Your fingers are gentle on my chin and I feel tears start as I look at you. I don't deserve gentleness and passion.

You pull me to my feet and kiss me again, carefully and slowly as if you know what I'm thinking. But when you pull away, I can see that you're not thinking about me any more. "I have to go, Kim. I have to think about what we're going to do. If Lassiter and his buddies have decided to go wolf hunting, we may have to take a little vacation before the next full moon. See if we can get the pack somewhere safer. First, I need to go talk to the rangers. You take care, hon. and I'll see you at the café later."

One last kiss and you're gone, leaving me to watch you walk away and swallow the lump in my throat. Your walk is strong and sure and you don't look back. I know from the set of your shoulders that you're balancing the safety of the pack against the safety of the town and I wish I could help you with it. Then I realize I can, in my own way.

But leaving is harder than I thought it would be. My car needs repairs, tips are short for a few days, a friend gets sick. I let these things hold me in place, tethering me when I know I should go. Before I realize it, the month slips past.

The hunters, Lassiter among them, come to the café and dream aloud of killing wolves. They speak in soft voices of wolves smarter than dogs, smarter even, maybe, than them. Wolves that are big, but slip away like shadows. Once I think I hear the word "silver," but then they all laugh and I think I must have imagined it.

I dream of pouring hot coffee on them, of burning them enough so that they cannot go to the woods, cannot harm the pack. Neither of us understands the other's dreams. But I hear from them that the rangers are alert and traveling through the woods looking for traps and it reassures me.

I linger until the night of the next full moon, knowing that I can't leave until I know you are safe from them at least. This time, we drive out of town in your truck before moonrise, not risking a walk through the woods. Your hands are sure on the wheel, your eyes far away as you scan for hunters. I look too, but don't see anything. Finally, when we have gone as far as we can before we change, you stop the truck on a deserted dirt road.

This time, we slink into hiding in the ditch before we change. You sniff the air around us before venturing out and I feel a flash of pure fury at the hunters who drove us to this. I follow you out and catch the faint scent of the pack on the wind. I yip quietly to catch your attention and together we follow it. We are quick but cautious, roaming in and out of cover and behind trees that reek of humans and metal.

Just as we reach the mountain, there is a volley of shots and a wolf's cry cut short. You surge ahead, running flat out up the mountain and I trail behind you, my heart hammering *No, no, no!* with each stride. We are close now, close enough to see the hunters surrounding the pack. You give one jump, landing hard on the back of the nearest hunter. He falls, his shot going wild and then I'm there too. We scatter them in the dark with fear and wild shots and sharp bites where we can find flesh, making an opening for the pack.

The other wolves flee and we turn to run after them. I am racing ahead of you when I hear the snap of steel jaws followed by your scream. I turn, snarling at the pack to keep running. They mill in confusion for a moment, then dart into the brush and away up the mountain. I charge back for you, pausing in the shadows when I see Lassiter. He wears a feral grin and he holds something out to you that gleams in the moonlight.

I shiver at my first sight of silver bullets. He knows. Beyond all reason and sanity, he knows what we are. For a moment, I think about running away with the pack, losing my human self in my wolf self out in the mountains. But you are here and you are in danger. I can no more leave you now than I could last month.

I make myself see the trap with almost human eyes. The teeth are closed around your paw, mangling your flesh. Lassiter is loading his gun and you are growling at him, a low, persistent terrifying sound that shakes the ground under me. I think about distracting him, about making a noise so he follows me but I can hear the other hunters now. He would just send one of them after me and stay here to shoot you.

There is only way to save you and I brace myself for what I must do. Lassiter points the gun at you, a twisted grin on his lips and you strain against the trap. You snarl, a last gesture of defiance as he fires, the silver bullets gleaming in the moonlight as I leap between their danger and you. I hear your anguished howl and my agonized whimpers as I drop to the snow. Somehow, you begin to change back to human. I see it as you leap over me, your half-human, half-wolf form finding the hunter.

He screams twice and then it is over. You are back at my side, not stopping to change from one form to another. I am drifting away, the silver poisoning my wolf self too quickly to be stopped. I see that your hand is mutilated by the trap's teeth and I try to lick it with the last of my strength. "Kimmeeee..." Your growl draws the word out.

At that moment, I know you love me and I am deliriously happy despite the pain. I see the anguish on your face as you shift back to sheriff to kiss me goodbye. Our lips meet and I give you one last not quite human smile as I slip away.

WAGE SLAVE

Andrea watched the new director sashay her way across the office and thought unkind thoughts. That skirt was way too tight, for one thing, and the silky blouse was too clingy. And then there were the heels. The less said about the way they stretched out her legs, making them look eight feet long at the same time that they made her stick out her round little ass as she walked, the better.

Andrea could feel her sense of righteous indignation burning its way up, well, pretty much every part of her body all at once. It had just made her nipples poke through her blouse and painted her cheeks a rosy pink when her boss brought the director over to introduce her. "And this is Andrea Anderson. She handles the bookkeeping, maintains the computer network and generally does whatever needs doing or fixing. Andrea, this is Sharon Wayne."

Sharon gave her a brilliant smile and reached over to shake her hand. Andrea took her hand reluctantly, trying not to glance down at the cleavage invitingly displayed at the top of Sharon's shirt. "Nice to meet you," she muttered through clenched teeth. It was just not fair.

"You too. I can always handle more doing and fixing, whenever you've got the time, Andrea." Startled, Andrea met Sharon's eyes for the first time. They were dark brown and seemed to bore right through her. *Even dyes her hair, the big phony* she nearly murmured out loud. Fortunately Bob swept Sharon off just about then. Just in time to give Andrea a spectacular view of the beautifully toned ass under the director's silky skirt.

Andrea stopped her fist before it went to her forehead in hopes of pounding some sense into her head. No point in being too obvious. Especially since it looked like Bob was going to do that for her. From this angle, it looked like he was trying to rub himself all over those very long legs in an act of desperate sincerity. Andrea pictured herself rubbing her way up those legs herself, perhaps licking and nibbling and…"Andrea! I can't login!" Sam was swearing at his computer again and she made herself forget Sharon, at least temporarily.

Since a few days passed before she saw Sharon again, it should have been easier to forget that first meeting. But somehow Sharon Wayne made herself at home in Andrea's dreams. She woke up one morning after a particularly vivid one about burying her face between Sharon's legs at one of those interminable quarterly meetings. Sharon tasted a little like honeyed mead, something that Andrea had sampled once at the local Medieval Faire. She spent her snooze time with her hand between her legs buried in her own soaking wet pussy, rubbing until she writhed with release.

That, of course, was the day that Sharon needed to get her computer logins and such set up. Andrea went in early, freshly showered and deodorized, no whiff of sex hanging around her like a cloud, no ma'am. She logged in and read the email that Bob sent her about getting the lock on Sharon's office door fixed before it locked her in. She shrugged and made a note to take care of it later. It wasn't like the overtime around here wouldn't have the same effect anyway.

Then she snuck over to Sharon's office and logged into her computer. She had finished the first round of installs and was focused on the second when a voice from the doorway made her jump. "My, my, someone's here early. Bob said you do an excellent job maintaining things around this place and I can see that he was right." Sharon was wearing pants today, along with heels and a blouse in some shimmery fabric that made Andrea's eyes go places that she didn't want them to.

Sharon dumped her jacket on the coat rack, dropping her bag in the process. That meant she had to bend over, exposing that perfect ass to Andrea's harassed gaze. Desperate to keep her hands and her mind to herself, Andrea murmured, "Thanks. It's nothing really. I'll be done in fifteen minutes if that's okay with you." She dragged her gaze back to the screen and forced her hands down on the keyboard, away from her lap and anything else they might potentially do on their own.

"That's just fine, hon. What are you doing anyway?" Sharon stepped around the desk and leaned against the back of the chair. Andrea's lungs filled with her scent and she squirmed a little as she got ever so slightly moist. Sharon brushed against her shoulder and she got a lot wetter. Soaked, really.

Sharon stayed where she was, didn't pull back an inch until Andrea couldn't stand it any more. Sure, installing the programs from the network instead of a CD would take longer but that was better than losing her job by making a pass at a straight director. "Just about done," she managed to choke out. "I can install the rest from the network so I'll just get out of your way."

She pulled herself out of the chair as if she was jet-propelled, ignoring Sharon's voice saying, "You weren't in the way--" as it trailed after her down the hallway. Hunting for shelter, she bolted into the single stall bathroom at the far end of the floor and locked the door behind her. Her hands fumbled with the zipper on her pants until she could drop them down around her ankles.

Then she slumped against the door, fingers buried in the hot wetness between her legs. She rubbed frantically, nearly convincing herself that Sharon was in the room with her until she came, thighs trembling with the effort it took to stay standing. Then there was nothing left to do but clean up, splash cold water on her face and hope she didn't run into Sharon again for a few days.

But no such luck. No sooner had she composed herself enough to leave the bathroom than she opened the door to find Sharon on the other side. "Oh there you are, Andrea. I was just going to say that I'll be in a meeting for a while this morning so feel free to finish installing in my office." She smiled and gave Andrea a look from those dark brown eyes that suggested that she knew just what the bookkeeper had been up to.

She vanished before Andrea could do more than turn beet red. She slunk back to Sharon's office and went to work. This time, she made the effort to look around at the photos and knickknacks the other woman had begun to unpack. There was a golf club on a desk organizer; surely that was a good sign. Andrea smiled to herself, noticing the lack of fluffy things on display, at least so far. At least until she got to the photos. There was Sharon with two kids and a dog, all smiling up at the camera, even the dog. Then there was the one with the tall good-looking guy with his arm around her, still smiling.

Andrea didn't smile back. This time, she did beat her fist against her forehead, but it didn't help. Sharon was entrenched, at least for the moment. And, just her luck, was walking through the door with that cheery smile from the photos plastered on her face instead of staying imaginary. Andrea pulled herself together and muttered, "Hi. You should be all set up. Here's your list of temporary passwords and your logins. Let me know if you have any trouble."

She tried to bolt out the door, only to find Sharon blocking the way. "Bob says you have the best grasp on the office expenses around here, Andrea. I was wondering if you could stay a little late on Thursday and explain them to me. I wouldn't ask that of you but you know how booked my schedule is."

Did those long blonde eyelashes flutter over those big brown eyes? Andrea couldn't be sure. She garbled something that could have been heard as agreement if that was what you wanted to hear and fled. Once around the corner, she paused to catch her breath. Alone in the office on Thursday night with Sharon? Her heart raced. She forced herself to be sensible: alone, except for the janitors and the security guard. How romantic.

It was only Tuesday now. She wondered if she'd manage to avoid making a fool of herself before Thursday rolled around. Then she wondered what would happen if she just brushed up against the director, by accident of course. Then she'd get to find out if those delicious curves were all they promised to be. Andrea began spending her lunch break in the bathroom or in her car, her hand between her legs imagining that her fingers were Sharon's tongue. She had never looked forward to Thursday with such a perfect mix of dread and anticipation before.

Then when Thursday finally dawned, it looked as if Sharon was going to have to reschedule. Andrea had to wait until lunchtime to find out for sure. Butterflies did exotic tropical dances in Andrea's stomach as she watched the clock. Had four hours always taken this long? She wasn't sure, but it just didn't seem right.

At last an instant message popped up: Sharon. Fingers trembling slightly, she clicked the little blinking icon. "Still on. Can I buy you dinner fr yr trble?"

She stared at the message as if it were going to grow fangs and attack her. Dinner? She couldn't possibly, she'd behave like an idiot, she'd get fired. Her fingers frantically typed: "I'll take a rain check on dinner, srry. C u at 5." There, that sounded all cool and professional, at least in IM speak. Now to make sure that the calm and collected Andrea was in charge at the end of the day. She pulled up her spreadsheets and went to work writing a report to show the director. Not the woman she wanted to make love to, but her boss's boss. Maybe if she told herself that enough times, it would sink in.

Five o'clock rolled around faster than should have been possible but by then Andrea thought she was ready. Sort of. She gathered up her various printouts and started for Sharon's office, waving her farewells as other people started to clear out. *Not deserted yet*, she noticed with a sigh of relief. It would be fine. She hoped.

Sharon was on the phone when she reached the office door, but she waved Andrea in and gestured toward the chair. From the tone of her voice, Andrea guessed that she was talking to one of her kids and resolutely tuned the conversation out. Still, she couldn't help but notice how firm Sharon's voice was. She wondered what it would be like for the director to speak just as firmly to her. She might order Andrea to do...*almost anything*. A tiny wet trickle ran from her pussy and over her labia. She tried not to scream in frustration.

Finally, Sharon got off the phone and turned her attention to her squirmingly aroused underling. Andrea wondered if she could smell desire from across the office. If she did, it didn't show. Instead, they looked at spreadsheets and figures for a while until Sharon had to step out for a minute. Andrea could hear the janitor vacuuming the cubicles outside and sighed with relief. They were almost done anyway.

That was the moment that Sharon stepped back inside, pulling the door closed behind her. The lock snapped shut with a finality that made Andrea jump. "Oh shit," she murmured before she could stop herself. Sharon's eyebrows rose and she reached back to try and open the door. It rattled but nothing else happened.

"My fault," Andrea volunteered. "I forgot to have this fixed. But we can just yell for Lee and he can get us out." She tugged at the door, feeling obliged to give it a try. Sharon's mild perfume swept over her in a wave and she nearly closed her eyes to breathe it in.

"Why don't we finish up first?" Sharon breathed. Standing this close to her, Andrea realized that she was a bit taller than the other woman. Her full lips were kissably close though, thanks to those heels she never took off. Her eyes were dark enough to fall into and her full, round breasts were so close that it was all Andrea could do not to reach out and take one in her hands. In fact, she checked out so far that for a moment, Andrea was terrified that she had done just that.

It wasn't until Sharon turned back toward the desk that she realized that her daydreams had simply gone too far. This had to stop. "So those are some cute kids you've got there. What does your husband do?" There, that would add the splash of ice water that she so desperately needed.

"Something with his boyfriend, generally, at least when he's not selling real estate." Sharon gave her a wicked smile, one that seemed full of hidden meanings. "We got divorced a few years back but managed to stay good friends. How about you, Andrea? Got any kids? Spouse or partner?"

She seemed weirdly relaxed for a woman who was locked in an office with a total stranger after 5. Andrea was baffled. Shouldn't one of them be calling for Lee before he left for the night? Of course, Jorge or Ana would be on duty at the security desk so they could just call down and ask to be rescued. That must be what she was thinking. She shook herself a little, reminding herself to stay in the moment before her worst fears came true. "Nope, no kids. Not married either." She gave Sharon what she hoped was a cheerful smile. "Now as for the expenses..."

Andrea rattled on for a bit, answering Sharon's questions while she wrote on the board behind Sharon's desk. It was almost enough to distract her, this discussion of areas where more money was needed and the places where they could cut back and save. She'd never been able to get Bob to listen to her like this; it was a nice feeling, and made her feel more optimistic about her job than she had in months.

Sharon chose that moment to walk up beside her to ask a final question about some specific point. Andrea glanced down and realized that she could see a lot more cleavage than she had when she'd come in. Sharon had definitely unbuttoned a bit. And wasn't there a bit more leg showing through that slit in her skirt? Sharon leaned in to point at something and brushed her breast against Andrea's arm, making the bookkeeper jump.

Once again, Sharon didn't step back, didn't apologize. Just went on looking Andrea straight in the eyes from way too close. Andrea stepped away only to find the wall at her back. She squirmed, fingers tugging at her collar to loosen it. She could feel a bead of sweat running down her neck, and a lot more than that sliding down between her thighs. Sharon looked impatient and asked her question again. She stepped in just a bit closer, well past comfort range and Andrea looked around frantically for a place to put her hands that wouldn't get her into trouble.

She'd settled on her pockets when Sharon caught her right hand in her own. "What a pretty ring!" The director turned a little so that her hip almost brushed Andrea's crotch. The bookkeeper let out a tiny moan, then tried to turn it into a cough. But it was too late. Sharon's smile told her all she needed to know. That was when the director reached up and unbuttoned the collar of Andrea's blouse. "Poor thing!" She purred. "You don't need to make yourself all hot and uncomfortable for me. I'm very impressed with your work and I suspect that'll continue. Don't you?"

Andrea nodded, not trusting herself to speak as those deft fingers withdrew from her collar. Sharon reached out and ran a finger through the line of sweat working its way down her neck. Andrea shuddered as Sharon licked her finger off. "I think," said the director, "that I know what will make both of us a bit more comfortable." She reached up and unbuttoned another button on her blouse, opening it enough so that Andrea could see the lacy top of her bra.

In another moment, she was going to be lost. She found her voice, somehow, dredged up the question that would drive away all the ambiguity. "Ms. Wayne, are you trying to seduce me?" She squeaked before closing her eyes, unable to bear the expression of shock and horror that was sure to greet it.

"Perhaps. Mostly I was hoping that you'd seduce me, Ms. Anderson."

Andrea's eyes flew open in shock. Sharon was still way too close, her shirt exposing far too much cleavage. Her eyes were filled with wry humor. "Unless you'd rather go on rubbing yourself off in the bathroom? Speaking of which, I wouldn't mind seeing your technique." Sharon slipped her hand between Andrea's legs and pressed up against her nearly molten pussy through her khakis.

Andrea closed her eyes and gasped for air as Sharon slowly unzipped and unbuttoned her pants. Sharon followed it up by running her hand down the center seam so that it disappeared briefly between Andrea's thighs. Andrea muffled a groan and drove her right hand into her own pants. Her fingers slipped in the thick wetness until she found her hardened clit. She barely touched it, circling the agonizingly sensitive flesh two or three times before she collapsed against the wall, thighs shaking.

"My, my," Sharon drawled in a patently fake Southern accent, "that was quite the show, darling." She fanned herself with one hand and pulled her shirt open to display ample cleavage trapped in a lacy bra.

That was the last straw: Andrea reached out and grabbed her. She pulled the other woman up and out of her heels for a bone-crushing kiss. She could feel Sharon unbuttoning her shirt and spun them both around so that Sharon's back was against the wall. Then she hoisted her up so that the director's legs were wrapped around her waist. Sharon moaned as Andrea tugged her shirt out of the waistband of her skirt, and did it again even louder when Andrea braced her with one arm and got her free hand inside her bra.

The full glories of Sharon's soft flesh rolled into her hand but Andrea realized that she wanted more. She tugged her hand loose from Sharon's bra then slipped it down between her legs. The director was wearing tiny, skimpy little underpants that were soaked all the way through. Andrea rolled them between her fingers and worked them up into Sharon's soaking wet slit. She rubbed the other woman's clit through the fabric with her thumb while she slid two of her other fingers inside her.

Sharon's eyes flew open and she spoke in that same tone of voice that she'd used on the phone. "I want you to eat me out now, Andrea."

Andrea knew an order when she heard one but that didn't mean she couldn't take her time following it. She spun around, maneuvering Sharon onto the edge of the desk. Then she leaned over to tongue Sharon's nipples into excruciating hardness through the lace of her bra until Sharon wailed. It was a sound of pure desire and it made Andrea grin as she tugged off the skimpy underwear. Here at least, she was in control and the world was as it should be.

That was when Sharon reached back and flipped the photos over before she turned around. "I'm not feeling any tongue where I want it, Andrea. I wouldn't want to have to ask Bob to put that on your next performance review." Andrea jerked her head up in alarm and looked at Sharon's face for reassurance. She didn't get much; Sharon raised one blonde brow and didn't smile. Andrea dropped to her knees and unbuttoned her skirt.

Her thoughts whirled as she ran her tongue gingerly up Sharon's bare thigh. What if she was serious? Would she have to spend all her spare time pleasuring her boss's boss? She squelched the thought and buried her face in the dark brown curls between Sharon's thighs instead. *I knew she dyed her hair.* The triumphant comment vanished into mumbled slurpings as the director's hands firmly dragged her face into her pussy.

She licked as if her job was at stake, though she hoped it wasn't. Her tongue caressed the hardening little knob of Sharon's clit like it was sugarcoated and she shoved a finger or two into the soaking wet pussy just beneath it. Sharon moaned, pulling the sound all the way up her torso and out her throat. Andrea noticed that she did taste a tiny bit like mead and licked harder, running her tongue from clit to slit, then back again. Sharon began to tremble, then to shake.

Her wails and moans stayed soft though, nothing that would alert the security guards as they made their rounds. Andrea stayed where she was as Sharon came, legs scissoring around her ears. She bent to her task again since the other woman's hands were still holding her face firmly in place. Maybe this would be worth a bonus. She ventured another finger inside the wet slit an inch under her nose.

This time, Sharon came so hard she nearly fell off the desk. Andrea managed to catch her before she got too far and the director fell backward on the desk instead, laughing. She finally released Andrea's head and the bookkeeper stood up, wiping her mouth with the back of her hand. Sharon pulled her up close and kissed her hard. She reached down and pinched Andrea's nipple through her shirt until it tore a groan from Andrea's throat. Andrea could feel her heart race, her breathing pick up until it sounded like she'd been running. She pulled Sharon in close, her hands frantically exploring the other woman's body.

Finally, Sharon pulled back, breaking off the kiss that threatened to make Andrea pass out. She pushed the bookkeeper gently back a few paces and gave her a loving look from under her dyed-blonde lashes. Then Sharon gave her a sunny smile and began buttoning her blouse and skirt. She stood up and tucked her underwear into Andrea's pocket and patted her cheek next to her open mouth. "So… same time next week, Andrea? I know I can count on you."

Without waiting for a response, she walked over and gave the door a good yank. It opened with a protesting squeal and she paused to blow Andrea an air kiss over one shoulder before she walked away, perfect ass swinging to the rhythm of her heels.

Heart's Thief

Ashara slipped through the window, pulling her hook and rope in behind her. The gesture came so easily it was as if she hadn't just had to climb the wall and pick the lock. All around her, the room was still and dark as an abyss and the night breeze sent a light shiver over her exposed arms. She wondered why she sensed no guards, no magical alarms.

After all, she had come for the Heart of El Kyraz, a ruby big as a man's fist. It was said that the stone had great powers if one had the strength to command it. Surely a gem merchant of Sher Kalia's status would at least have mortal guards to protect such a jewel. Rumor held that she'd had one of the most famous wizards in the city as her lover. She'd have asked for wards, have asked him to send the cold blue light of his power around her most cherished possessions. The price of such protection would have been nothing more than pillow talk to someone as wealthy as Kalia.

And yet there was nothing, not so far. She strained her senses as far as she could in the stillness, then accepted defeat. If there were wards here, her limited magic could not find them. Pulling a small stone from her pocket, she whispered a charm over it. The rock took on a pale green glow, bright yet not enough to light the room. She tossed it to the floor a few steps away, then pulled out another one and repeated the charm.

Soon a line of the small stones cast their pale glow in a path across the deserted room, at least as far as the bolted door in the wall opposite.

Ashara stepped forward carefully, gathering up the stones as she went. Their light winked out when they vanished into her pocket but it would take only a word to set them aglow again. Old Mirean had done his work well.

She almost smiled, the way she did when there was no one around to see the way it twisted the long scar that ran from temple to chin down her thin face. Best not to think on how grotesque it made her appear. Best to look as if she thought nothing, felt nothing. No one shrank away from her in the market then. She wrinkled her nose, an old pain flitting across her features.

Of course, if she were caught here, the Governor would hang her and there would be no more worries about her looks. She reached the door as just as the thought crossed her mind and it was enough to make her pause and hesitate. But it was too late now. She could be hung merely for being here, even if she took nothing. Better to die trying or better yet live to succeed and to leave the city of El Kyraz.

She wrapped the bolt on the door with the rags she'd brought with her for that purpose. Again she whispered a few words, then tugged gently. The bolt came away in her hands as silently as a sigh. That left only the lock. She reached into her pockets and produced several small tools and one of the stones. She let it glow just enough so she could see to work and picked the door's lock as if she'd been born to it.

For a moment, she wondered if this might be easier if she had. The children of the thieves' clans seemed much more skilled than she. She had only her training from Mirean, nothing more. Yet here she was, opening the door to the treasure vault in one of the richest merchants' homes in the city. This time, she did smile and thought nothing of whether or not it improved her looks. Then she opened the door a crack so that she could peer inside.

A loud persistent hum from the room beyond made her shut the door immediately, heart racing in terror. She stood still, waiting for some unknown power to attack her from the other room, every limb straining to flee for a span of breaths. One, two, then a third.

Still nothing. She forced herself to open the door again, this time wide enough for her lean form to slip inside.

Now she could see the source of the sound: it came from a series of shining red stones perched on stone pillars along the wall. They were surrounded by locked chests but Ashara paid no attention to these. She had not come for lesser treasure. She studied the stones on their pillars and her jaw fell open in amazed horror for an instant. Sher Kalia had earned her reputation for ingenuity: the merchant had hidden the Heart among multiple false hearts.

She stood motionless in front of them, trying to sense something, anything that would tell her which one was the right one. After what seemed an eternity, she thought she could feel a spark, a whiff of magic. She scanned the row of stones again. There, that one on the far end, it felt different from the others. She approached it cautiously, wondering what kind of unseen guards the merchant had added to this room.

Soon she was a few steps from it and there she stopped, waiting for a sign of some sort. This stone, or rather the gold she could sell it for, would buy her way free. Always provided it was the right one. No more indenture to Mirean. No more fleeing from her stepfather's fists and knife through the market place. She would take her coin and run far away from all of it. Perhaps in Caldos or Ondas, she could find a sorcerer who could heal her face. Or maybe even someone who would love her in spite of it.

She stepped closer, reaching into her bag for the special charm that Mirean had given her for the moment when she found the Heart. Slowly she reached out and held it above the red gem. She could see it pulse in the glow of her stone now, its center seeming to beat in some strange trick of the light. She reached for it with her other hand, moving cautiously until her fingertips barely stroked its surface.

The resulting shock threw her across the room, causing her to drop her glow stone and Mirean's charm. She collided with the stone wall opposite the Heart with an exquisitely painful jolt before dropping to her knees on the floor. As she lay gasping for air, there was a whisper of a door opening and the faint scruff of soft slippers on the stone floor. Torches lit around the chamber with a low pop. A slender foot appeared under her nose, causing her to recoil backwards as if from a snake. "Did you think my Heart would be so easy to take, little thief?"

She looked up into Sher Kalia's face and cringed. Not that the merchant looked cruel or even angry. On the contrary, her face was beautiful: all dark eyes and ebony skin, full lips pursed as if for a kiss. Under other circumstances, Ashara would have admired her beauty and sighed at the knowledge that such a one would never look at her. Now she shrank away, eyes wide with terror at her probable fate.

"So young to bear the mark of the blade," Kalia murmured as she bent over and ran a single cool finger down the scar on Ashara's cheek. "Certainly too young to have entered here on your own unaided." She cupped Ashara's chin in her hand and tilted her face up so that Ashara's eye met her own. And were swallowed by them. The merchant's eyes were demon-dark and night sky deep and the young thief could no more look away than she could fly.

Somehow, she remembered words and forced them to her lips. Discarding the ones that pleaded for her life, she selected from among the others. "What are you going to do to me?" A distant part of herself was pleased that her voice scarcely trembled.

"What do you think I should do to you, little thief?" Kalia's hand tugged upward, pulling Ashara to her feet with the pressure. "The Heart approves of you or you would have died when you touched it. That is something. What else can you do besides steal?"

Ashara paused, studying the merchant from under lowered lids. Her long robes draped themselves over sweet curves and her lips held promises that the thief longed to hear. Greatly daring, she murmured, "I can perform some household magics, lady. I can make you laugh. And...," she hesitated a moment before she continued. "I can please you, lady. I can give you your heart's desire."

Sher Kalia threw back her head with a shout of startled laughter. "You promise so little, small thief! How would a baby scavenger like you know anything of what my heart desires?" Her eyes narrowed in amusement as she studied Ashara's face, her fingers never releasing their burning hold on her chin.

Ashara took a deep breath, then let it out slowly as she closed her eyes. She reached out with all the power in her, stretching until she could touch Kalia's mind with her own. There…there it was. A memory so strong that it tasted like a sweet wine to her mind. She embraced it until it sent a wave of heat through her, lapping at her thighs and making her gasp. Eyes still closed, she reached for Kalia, pulling the merchant's face down to her own and kissing her with all of that memory in her mouth, her tongue.

Now it was the merchant's turn to gasp even as her body molded itself to Ashara's lean length. Ashara could feel the surprised desire fill the other woman's body until her blood ran hot with it and she very nearly smiled. But that might break the illusion, might remind her that she held not the beloved of her past but a scrawny stranger instead. And Kalia had never known a woman's touch before. She must go cautiously. A single misstep might cause her power to fail and drive the other woman to call for her guards. Then she would send Ashara to the gallows.

Greatly daring, she touched her mind to Kalia's, reminding the other of the pleasure she had known. As the merchant's lips parted in a tiny moan, she broke off the kiss to trail her lips and tongue down Kalia's flesh to where her robe dipped above her breasts. She glanced upward in time to see the merchant's eyes close and her head tilt back. A gasp of pleasure escaped her lips as Ashara reached out to take her breast in her mouth.

Her pleasure ran through Ashara like a bolt, making her knees tremble and her thighs slick with it. The thief pulled the merchant closer, her mouth hot and wet on all she could reach of Kalia's exposed flesh. Ashara's fingers reached for the sash around Kalia's waist, opening the knot and tugging it apart as deftly as she had picked the lock to the merchant's house.

Kalia moaned as her robe fell open and Ashara's mouth met her overheated flesh. Then her own fingers seized handfuls of the thief's tunic, tugging it loose and over her head. She caught Ashara's face in her hands and tilted it up to her own, wide eyes searching the thief's. That was when Ashara realized that Kalia's lover was gone forever, killed in a sorcerous battle across the sea. The grieving emptiness that filled the merchant threatened to overwhelm her thoughts and her mind spun, trying to free herself from the web of power she had built between them.

The merchant's eyes opened then, as if she could somehow feel Ashara's efforts to escape. Her dark eyes met the thief's and a single tear rolled down her cheek. Ashara froze, letting Kalia's sorrow wash over her in a wave. The two women stood, arms wrapped around each other, seemingly lost in each other's gaze for a span of heartbeats.

Kalia spoke first. "Perhaps you cannot give me my heart's desire after all, little thief." She raised her hand and ran her thumb along Ashara's jaw with a sigh. Then she began to pull away and Ashara could feel herself being shut off from that awful pain.

"No!" She yelped the word from instinct alone, reaching out to clutch the merchant's open robe with quick desperate hands. "Let me try. I think I can...help you." It was the fear of a thief's death at the end of a rope that drove her words. She knew that it could be nothing more. Well, that and perhaps a bit of pity for the one who carried such a burden.

Kalia gave her a long look, as if considering whether or not a fledging scavenger could replace her heart's beloved, even for a few hours. Through the web that still remained between him, Ashara could feel her desire, still present and running like a river beneath her skin. She reached out and coaxed it just a little, just enough so that she could smell it rising from between the merchant's legs. She did not smile, waiting instead with her hands on the other's waist for what she would say next.

The merchant pulled her close and kissed her hard, full lips engulfing her narrow ones as Kalia's tongue sought her own. Then she broke away and seized Ashara's hand. Tugging the thief with her, she walked purposely from the room where the red gems watched them and into the hallway beyond.

She did not close her robe or insist that Ashara cover herself so the thief gratefully assumed that the servants and guards were asleep at this hour. Or at least she prayed to all her gods that they were asleep. The web was not so strong that an interruption couldn't break it, reminding Kalia in full force that the woman she led down the corridor was an intruder, bent on taking what was hers.

But they met no one before Kalia stopped at a door of studded timber, the imported wood alone worth more than all of Ashara's possessions put together. *Perhaps I should take it instead of the Heart.* Ashara's lips twisted into the beginnings of a wry smile as she imagined herself carrying the huge heavy door away from the merchant's palace and giving it to Mirean in place of the gem.

The thought vanished as Kalia pushed the door open to reveal a richly furnished bedchamber lit by a few sputtering candles. A huge bed hung with silky curtains stood in the middle of the room, all the other furnishings fading to insignificance beside it.

When the merchant looked at it, Ashara could feel something in her link with Kalia, some increase in longing and pain that made her bite her lip to stop from responding to it. Kalia gave her a sidelong glance. "Can you make yourself look like him?" Her tone was cool and emotionless, with only the pain humming beneath it to suggest that the question had any significance.

Ashara shook her head, wondering whether or not to tell the merchant the nature of the link between them. Finally she settled on a piece of the truth. "I can make you feel something, something like what you felt in the past as long as I can feel what you feel." Even as she spoke, she wondered if it was even part of the truth. Would her powers work on the merchant if the woman felt no desire for her?

"And how will this help me?" Kalia released her hand and paced slowly toward the bed, stopping at a table where a jar of wine sat open. She poured some into two cups and offered the second one to Ashara. The thief took a nervous gulp of its contents while she considered the question and the striking curves of the merchant's body now clearly displayed by her open robe. Kalia ran a hand over her belly then reached up to cup her breast. One thumb stroked her nipple into hardness as she watched Ashara.

Ashara's words caught in her throat and Kalia smiled and slipped the robe off, dropping it to the floor. She reached down into the glistening wet darkness between her legs with her other hand, caressing the folds of her flesh until it felt as if she was touching Ashara herself.

The thief trembled, her feet lurching forward in a single step, hesitating, then lurching forward again. Now it felt as if the merchant controlled the web that linked them, but that was impossible. Somewhere in Ashara's mind, a voice told her to flee from the unknown, to run away from this unbearably lovely woman with the sad, sad eyes. To deny her desperate longing to touch and be touched.

She managed to set the cup aside as Kalia moaned. Her fingers moved on her flesh more briskly now, as if she'd forgotten the thief was still there. Ashara was close enough to touch her now and she reached out a fearful hand to touch the merchant's bare breast. Then she dropped to her knees before Kalia, sliding her tongue between the other woman's fingers to taste her musky sweetness. Kalia threw her head back as Ashara slipped her own fingers inside her and her tongue caressed her wet folds.

The merchant's hand retreated as she tried to support herself on the small table. It shuddered in her grasp so she chose instead to fall backward onto the bed, her feet remaining on the floor and Ashara's mouth between her legs. Ashara held on, her tongue lapping at Kalia's flesh as the merchant wailed, a low strained tone of frantic need.

The sound sent chills through Ashara, making her fingers thrust harder to change the rhythm of the merchant's desire. To make her feel anything more than the remembered anguish that she felt now. Kalia's back arched, her body bucking around Ashara's fingers as she clutched at the silken blankets.

Then she lay still, gasping for her breath in little choked sobs. Ashara reached out again, feeling her way along the web of Kalia's memories until she found what she was looking for. But she hesitated to take them up, instead looking warily at the merchant. "Do you want me to go?"

Tears rolled down Kalia's face until she wiped them fiercely away. "No." The word was almost a snarl as she reached out and pulled Ashara up on the bed beside her. Her hands were rough on the thief's body as she tugged her remaining garments off. "You know too much about me, little thief. Tell me something of yourself while I discover some of what *your* heart desires."

Ashara moaned as the merchant's teeth found the tender flesh of her breast, her tongue soothing the marks away an instant later. "I'm an apprentice to…" She managed to stop herself from saying Mirean's name aloud as Kalia thrust her leg between her own. "A thief, one of the clans." She gasped this last, relieved that she'd managed to lie enough to spare the old man a death by the rope. He, at least, had been kinder to her than her own family and deserved better.

"Indeed. I don't believe you, little one." Kalia's fingers thrust their way suddenly into Ashara's waiting wetness, making her buck against them. Almost without meaning to, she rode their pressure, Kalia's mouth seemingly everywhere all at once, licking and biting. Alternately trembling with fear and desire, Ashara wailed, her body convulsing around Kalia's fingers and tongue.

The merchant moved suddenly, twisting so that Ashara was pinned beneath the hot silkiness of her flesh and the bed beneath her. The merchant's mouth was fire on her own and Ashara slipped a little further along the web that linked their memories. For a moment, she was Kalia's beloved and her eyes were filled with the ghost of remembered love. For a moment, Kalia was the lover she dreamed of, the one who would see her as beautiful despite her scarred face. In that moment, too, she was master of the Heart and knew the secrets of the wards that held it in place.

But it was too much and she broke free at the other woman's next words, shivering in reaction as their link was lost. "What's the scar from, thief?" Kalia's lips thinned and she trapped Ashara's limbs with her own as the smaller woman bucked and writhed her efforts to get free. Finally, she sagged into the bed, realizing the futility of her struggles.

She closed her eyes, shutting out Kalia's face with an effort. "It was a 'gift' from my mother's husband. He gets drunk and he hurts us, my sisters and me. Once I was too slow. I will not be so slow again." She opened her eyes, letting the rage inside her meet the grief in Kalia's along the tendrils of their connection.

This time, she felt the merchant reach back, sending a wave of cold fury at the wizard who slew her beloved. At her beloved for fighting a magical duel at all. Then she felt the death of the other wizard, felt a tendril of magic so wrong that she recoiled in shock.

For a moment, she could see his death, see him disappear with a scream while Kalia raised the Heart high above her head, its fatal rays gleaming around her. The realization that the gem could be used for death magic shook Ashara to her core. Perhaps Mirean's desires were not so clear as they seemed; he must know what the gem could do in the wrong hands. Death magic was so forbidden that immediate execution awaited those who were caught attempting it. Kalia's life would be forfeit if anyone found out that she merely knew such powers, let alone had used them.

She felt something more in Kalia: a cold pain, a loathing for what she had done with the power of the Heart. The merchant's voice broke into her thoughts. "The thief clans do not train their minds this way." Kalia's lips twisted. "Now tell me who you really are, little thief and why you chose my home to rob." She settled her body down on Ashara's, so close that the thief gasped for breath, desire choking her thoughts.

Ashara scrambled for words. Would the merchant simply kill her to keep her secret? It would be easy enough to accomplish, helpless as she way. Still, Kalia's flesh called an answering song from her own, letting her thighs grow slick and wet with it. She wanted the merchant's fingers inside her again, her tongue on her flesh.

Kalia ground her ample hips against Ashara's narrow ones and ran her tongue up the thief's neck. She smiled when Ashara wailed and squirmed, her body begging for things that her lips would not. "Just tell me, little thief. I won't hurt you and I won't give you to the Governor's Guard. I merely want to know who knows so much about me."

Ashara surrendered, craving Kalia's touch. "My master was once a merchant like yourself until he fell from the Governor's favor. He wants the Heart to return him to the wealth he knew." Ashara rocked her hips a little in hopes of displacing the merchant. Any more of this, and she would answer any question the other woman asked without meaning to.

"Hmm…that would be Old Mirean, wouldn't it? No, don't bother to deny it. I can feel the truth in you." Kalia looked thoughtful. But her voice was cold and it boded no good to Mirean. "How foolish of him. The Heart chooses its own master. He cannot bargain it away like a bauble in the marketplace."

"Is that how you got it?" Ashara whispered the question, almost too fearful to ask it at all.

"It was a gift from my beloved. It accepted me on a day that I still curse. My lover died trying to protect it and I died with him, died enough to use its powers against his slayer." Kalia's eyes burned with the memory and the emptiness inside her almost swept Ashara away with it. "I protect it because it is what I have left of him. Mirean will do no better with it than I have."

Ashara's thoughts raced frantically. She was torn. Perhaps she could distract the merchant enough to escape and warn her master. But then why should she? Would he kill her himself if he thought she knew about the gem's powers? Uncertainty filled her but she found that desire was stronger. Squirming, she reached up and kissed Kalia's full lips, the touch of her mouth hot on the other woman's.

It was enough to distract the merchant. Kalia shifted so that her plump thigh thrust its way between Ashara's, smiling at the thief's gasp. She nuzzled Ashara's ear, her teeth nipping the tender skin. The little thief rocked her moist slit against Kalia's leg, groaning as a wave of heat spread its way through her. Kalia's hand found her breast and pinched the tender skin into hardness as Ashara's back arched away from the bed. Her body shook as bolt after bolt shot through her, leaving her breathless and collapsed beneath the merchant's curves. Kalia's eyes locked with hers and she knew the merchant was no threat to her.

In a moment Ashara realized what she must do. She reached out with all her power, diving effortlessly through the merchant's memories, searching for one that she could use. She found it in the last quarrel the merchant had had with her lover before he left for beyond the sea. Relentlessly, she dragged it to the surface of the merchant's mind, letting the other woman relive it. Ashara held her tight, soothing the anguish as it rose, allowing it to ebb away through the web that linked them. Carefully, she did the same with some of Kalia's other memories until the merchant shut her eyes and rolled away, her face wet with tears.

Almost Ashara wept with her as she released the web that bound them together, horrified that she had caused such pain, Then she reached for the merchant, letting her mouth and hands convey what she wanted to say. She explored Kalia's body with nimble fingers and tongue, caressing and coaxing until the merchant trembled with pleasure and release. They held each other, flesh pressed to flesh until Kalia's eyes closed in sleep, her breathing slowing. The little thief planted a soft kiss on her lips and smiled down at her, the expression lighting her face until it seemed whole.

Then Ashara rose silently from the bed. Gathering her clothes, she crept forward until she reached the door. She turned to glance at Kalia's face, watching old pain slip away like the tide. Then Ashara turned, still smiling and slipped through the barely opened door. She pulled her clothes on as she went, glancing from side to side for early-waking servants and guards.

The room stood as open as they had left it, she and Kalia, and the multiple Hearts sat waiting on their pedestals. She pulled her tunic back on before she turned confidently to the stones. This time, she knew which one to choose and walked toward it without glancing at the others.

She paused before it for a long moment, thinking about what she would do with the powers of such a gem at her command. She imagined a palace in Ondas, one near the sea where her sisters and her mother could come and live with her. She imagined Mirean restored to his old life so that he did not pursue her. Then she imagined Kalia healed and able to love once more.

Then she murmured the words she had heard in the merchant's mind, releasing the wards before she reached for the gem. This time when she touched it, there was no shock. The stone came up into her hands as if it greeted an old friend and her heart sang a little.

Ashara placed the Heart of El Kyraz into her pack and slipped silently from the treasure chamber. She didn't think Sher Kalia would miss it and she smiled at the thought as she made her way out and away from the city.

Blind Faith

I could tell Janet was freaked out when she came by. Her dark blue eyes were wide, like she was staring at something I couldn't see and her hands trembled as she walked past me, yanking off her jacket on the way.

As if all that wasn't enough, she was here on a day that wasn't one of "our" days. Her steady sweetie, Al, wasn't going to be thrilled about that, not like that was the most important thing going here. Deal with the drama later, that's my motto. Or I'd like it to be, if I had one. Still, it would've given me a little bit of rush, like doing something forbidden, if she hadn't looked so upset.

I watched her drop into the only big chair in my little apartment. She didn't say a word, just sat there and stared at me. Now I was getting seriously worried; normally she'd be talking a mile a minute, upset or not. I plopped down onto the footstool in front of her and took her hands. "What's the matter, babe?"

Tears started pouring down her cheeks. I was holding her in my arms when she mumbled into my ear, "I'm going blind, Linda. The tests came back positive. They say there's nothing they can do to stop it."

I went cold all over but I made myself hang on. Janet was an artist, a painter and illustrator; the news didn't get any worse than this. She mumbled something about what the doctors called it and how much longer she had before her vision went but that part went right past my dazed brain.

Being a selfish asshole, I started thinking about what this was going to mean for me, or for our relationship anyway. She was going to need lots of support over the long haul and everything was going to change. I suddenly realized that I had my doubts that I was the kind of gal who'd stick around for that. I mean, I liked Janet a lot but part of what I liked was that dealing with the day-to-day events in her life wasn't my problem. I was around for kicks and laughs and most of the time that was okay by me. Couldn't say that the realization felt too good just then.

She pulled away a little bit like she could read my mind. Then she looked up at me with those big blue eyes and it was like she could see right through me to the good and the bad and the ugly in my little reptile brain. I looked away after a minute, not ready for her to see what a fuckup I was. Finally she said, "I'm sorry to dump this on you. Al's out of town on a business trip and I just really needed to tell someone. Text messages don't cover it." Her beautiful, kissable lower lip quivered and another tear rolled down her face.

I kissed her as hard as I could, my heart in my mouth so to speak. I made it long and deep and engulfing and she kissed me back like she was drowning and I was her only lifeline. I knew then that she wasn't just here to talk. She needed to know I'd be there for her and I couldn't answer that part yet, but she also needed to know that someone still wanted her, no matter what. At least I hoped that was part of what was going on since I figured I was good for that much. I held her tight and murmured her name. Then I made another misstep. "Baby, you're beautiful. It won't make a difference in how anyone sees you—"

"What the hell are you talking about, Linda? Don't you understand what's going on here? Everyone's going to see poor blind Janet who used to be an artist. Everything from this point onward is going to be about people feeling sorry for me. Hell, about me feeling sorry for me. What part of this isn't making sense to you?"

"I'm sorry, I'm sorry. It's kind of a shock to me too, you know. I'm gonna say the wrong thing for a while." The kiss had left me wanting more, wanting to bury my face between her legs and show her that I could still offer what I always had. But now I was pissed off and defensive too. Of course, I didn't get it. I mean, blind was a big deal. And it wasn't like it had ever happened to me.

She was quiet for a few minutes, then she mumbled, "Yeah, I know. Maybe I should go home, call my folks and Al instead. I know you're not ready for this." She pulled away, her shoulders heavy with pain and I realized that I was a complete shit.

That was something I was even less ready to admit. "No, babe. C'mn, I can do better than that. Do you want a beer or something to eat? Maybe some tea? Just lean back and get comfy and let me take care of you for a little while." She gave me a tiny smile, pure terror lurking in the back of those eyes that I loved looking into. I wondered if I'd like it as much if I knew they weren't looking back. Then she nodded so I decided to fill in the blanks and headed for the kitchen.

Once there, I threw a bunch of stuff together on a tray while I brewed up some raspberry tea. The package said it was soothing and who was I to argue with the local coop's advertising? In the meantime, I grabbed some fruit, some chocolate, soft cheese, anything I could get my hands on. Part of me wanted to drag it out, to stay in the kitchen as long as I could get away with it, anything to avoid dealing with Janet. I told that part of me to shut the hell up and rocketed back out as soon I thought the tea was done.

Janet smiled a little more when I handed her the teacup, and the smile almost reached her eyes when she saw the jumbled mess of food on the tray. "You forgot the crackers," she said but then she grabbed my arm before I could go track them down. "No, wait. Just sit with me for a little bit, Linda. I need to talk."

I sat and held her hand and she told me about everything she was afraid of: that she'd never be an artist again, that her whole life would change for the worse, that no one would love her. That Al and I would both bail, which was the thing that caught me off guard. Sure, I was a loose cannon but Al was steady as a rock, always there in a crisis. Or so I'd thought up till now. Maybe I didn't get them as well as I thought. I didn't interrupt though, since it seemed like it all needed to come out.

I was staring at her feet and listening when I had an idea. She had stopped talking for a couple of minutes, lips still parted so I popped a strawberry in her mouth. She closed her eyes, savoring the flavor. I could see her smile a little and that made me smile back for the first time since she came over. She swallowed and I tapped her lower lip with a piece of chocolate. She took it without opening her eyes, enjoying it the same way that she had the strawberry.

I had another idea but I wasn't sure that it was as good as the first one. I gave it a few more minutes to see if she was going to say anything more or if I was going to come up with something brilliant that was going to make it all better. No such luck. I rubbed some soft cheese on a slice of cucumber and fed it to her while I thought about it.

I decided that I might as well take my chances. "Babe, I'd like to show you how special you are if you're up for it. I was thinking we could try it with a blindfold on, just to get an idea of what it'll be like. And use some of the food too." I stopped when I saw the look on her face. Clearly I still wasn't getting it.

"What, so I can practice? I'm going to have the whole rest of my life for practice!" She looked from me to the food and her face changed. I flinched, waiting for her to tell me we were through. But trust Janet to do the unexpected. "Unless you're willing to wear the blindfold?"

I hesitated for about the time it took to draw a breath. Bottoming just isn't my thing but a gal's gotta make exceptions. She needed to run this show, that much was obvious. It wouldn't kill me to try something new. I nodded my head like it was on strings. At least it wouldn't involve me saying much and that seemed to be a really good idea.

She gave me a twisted grin and got up to go into the bedroom. I followed her with the tray. By the time I got in there, she was pulling the silk scarves out of the drawer. I had a flash of her tied to the bed with them while I trailed my tongue down her naked body and felt myself get damp with anticipation. I tried to switch our bodies around in my head but that got distracting fast. Best to just go with it.

Janet patted the bed invitingly. She had a glint in her eyes that made me nervous. It was the last thing I saw as she wrapped the scarf around my eyes. She tied it nice and snug and made it broad enough that I couldn't see a thing under or over it. Then she popped a piece of chocolate into my mouth. Something about concentrating on chewing made it a little sweeter, made it melt in my mouth just a bit faster.

Or maybe that was the feel of her hands as she unbuttoned my shirt. I started to reach for her and she smacked my hands down lightly. Then she kissed me, sliding her tongue into my mouth for the last of the chocolate. I could feel her breathing get a little faster as she got the last of the buttons undone and pulled my shirt off. She ran her lips and tongue down my neck, then bit my shoulder just hard enough to get my attention.

Another cucumber slice coated in soft cheese turned up at my lips and I took it from her fingers, savoring the weird crunchy texture. She reached around me to unsnap my bra and I leaned forward into her breasts, kissing them through the fabric of her t-shirt. She stayed there long enough for me to work my mouth down to her nipple, but once it started getting hard, she pushed me away and down onto the bed.

Now I could feel myself breathing faster too. I wanted to feel her naked body pressed up against mine, with no visual distractions to take away from how hot it felt. I guess she wanted something like that too from the way that she was unzipping my jeans: fast and competent like nothing was going to stand in her way. Then she pulled them off, taking my underwear with it. I could feel one finger brush against my wet bush and I squirmed a little, hoping to get more.

No such luck. Instead she grabbed my arms and started pulling me up the bed. I went along with it, pushing myself with my feet until she could get the first of the scarves wrapped around one wrist then the other, securing me to the bed posts. *So this was what it felt like* I thought, testing her knots with my arms. I was still hot for her but now I was starting to feel helpless and I didn't like that part so much.

Janet stuck a hand between my legs and popped a strawberry inside all the wetness that was just aching for something more substantial. It got another strawberry, then two. Then something a little lumpier: chocolate. I stopped testing the scarves; maybe this would be more fun than I expected.

She got off the bed and I couldn't tell what she was doing, other than not touching me, which was the important part. I squirmed, feeling the strawberries jostle around and the chocolate start to melt around them. I could smell them now, getting all ground up with my own scent and it was getting me a lot hotter. I made an impatient noise, hoping to hurry her back from wherever she'd gone. I could hear her chuckle from somewhere nearby and I pictured her just sitting there watching me, blindfolded and spread-eagle on the bed with chocolate oozing out of my pussy.

Vulnerable. I think that was the word for what I was feeling. I liked it and hated it all at the same time. What if I didn't look so hot this way? What if she just decided to untie me and leave? I made a noise, something between a moan of frustration and longing. She giggled and sounded just like her usual self for a minute. I started to feel better.

That was when I realized that I was starting to get it, just a little. If we were going to stay together, I was going to have to learn a few things and today was just the beginning. Well, I thought that might be all right by me. Probably. I opened my mouth to say so. She popped in another piece of cucumber before I could say a word and I decided it could wait.

She climbed onto the bed next to me and from the way her skin felt when she brushed against me, she was naked too. And she smelled good, all lavender-scented lust with an aftertaste of strawberries. Speaking of taste, I wondered what I'd have to do to get her to ride my face. The chocolate-strawberry cocktail between my legs got oozier. Janet rubbed something on my tit, then started it licking it off. This time, I did moan, letting it all out.

She ate whatever it was off my boob, then smeared something on the other one. It was cool, then hot under her tongue, like there was a direct line between that patch of skin and my clit. My pussy was starting to ache now, throbbing until it took over my brain. I said a word I'd never used in bed with her before: "Please…"

"'Please' what, baby? Oh, I know - you want more chocolate!" She stuck another piece in my mouth and a second one into the oozing mess between my legs. I squirmed against her hand, trying as hard as

I could to get her fingers on my clit. She giggled and trailed something sticky down my ribcage. Her tongue followed it, moving as slowly as possible and leaving me with nothing to think about except how that felt.

She did it again, this time rubbing her breasts against whatever it was and using them to spread it around. My whole body was starting to tingle like every nerve was awake. I caught my breath every time she touched me, getting hotter and hotter by the minute until she finally worked her way down to my thighs.

Then she switched to my feet, licking and sucking on each patch of skin like it was the most important thing in the world. I spread my legs and squirmed and wailed with every inch, like that was going to move things along any. But by then I didn't care. I just wanted her to take me, to make me come until I couldn't do it any more. And I wanted it now.

Her tongue found my clit and it was like an electric jolt lifting me off the bed. My back arched and I tugged at the scarves as hard as I could, feeling the knots give just a little. But not enough to set me free. She buried her face in my pussy, pulling out a chocolate-covered strawberry with her tongue. Then a second one, following by a swipe against my clit with a tongue made even softer with melted chocolate. I came hard then, bucking against a third swipe of her tongue. I could feel the last of the strawberries get crushed inside me and the smell filled the room while I twisted and shook.

Janet purred like a cat against my clit and sucked out the last of the strawberry mush. Then she started swiping her tongue through me, cleaning me out like I was a big bowl of cream until I was begging for her hand inside me, no her fist. I wanted to take in everything I could and feel her take me on a ride like we'd never done it before. She shoved two fingers inside me and I rode them like a rodeo champ. Then four and I took them in like they were part of me. When she put her whole hand in and clenched the fingers together, I howled and twisted until one of the scarves finally tore.

But I kept my hand where it was until she pulled it free of the rags. This was her scene as much as mine and for the first time in my life, I liked giving in. She kissed my fingers and untied my other hand. Then she pulled off the blindfold and let me blink my way back to seeing the room, the chocolate smeared sheets and her blue eyes looking down at me with a very serious expression. I got worried for a second until she said what was on her mind, "What'll we do when strawberries are out of season?" I laughed and pulled her close. Maybe I could be a part time rock after all.

THE PARTY

Ana paced nervously around her small bedroom and tried not to look at Frida. She always seemed so intense. Ana risked a peek. Frida looked back and so did the small monkey on her shoulder. She wondered if the real Frida Kahlo would have gone to a sex party. Ana had heard she was pretty wild. But she still felt pretty dumb thinking about talking to a poster, even though it was almost as good as talking to the cats sometimes. At least since Sue left.

Of course if she hadn't left, Ana wouldn't be sitting there all queasy and just a little bit wet thinking about tonight. Nope, she'd be settling in for a big night of videos and popcorn...Maybe Max had a point when she told Ana that Sue splitting with the dyke from UPS was the most interesting thing that her ex was likely to do. Sue hadn't liked Max, either, the few times they met. Softball dyke meets butch top social worker. It got ugly.

Maybe that was why Ana liked Max almost at once. She said exactly what she thought. If she'd been dating Max, she would have known about Ms. UPS before anything happened, if nothing else. Not that she would have been dating Max, of course. All that leather stuff was fun to fantasize about, but she was pretty sure she wasn't ready to try it. Still, when Max invited her to go to this thing tonight, she'd agreed. It was almost six months since Sue left, and Ana knew that everyone was tired of her moping around. So she was going, but just to make them happy.

She stared mournfully into her closet. What the hell did you wear to these things, anyway? The white turtleneck with the little flowers? Definitely not. Not the vast collection of crucifixes on chains that her family had foisted off on her since she came out, either. They made her feel like a vampire. She continued toward the back of the closet, shaking her head. The little black wool dress? Too formal, and probably the wrong kind of hot, when she stopped to think about it.

Finally she settled on the red silk shirt with the buttons, the one she hoped she'd have the nerve to wear without a bra, and a short, full black skirt. Easy access, she thought, and blushed, laughing at herself in the mirror on the back of the closet door. At least she looked pretty cute. The red shirt set off her cocoa butter complexion, and she posed, modeling the outfit. Plainly, it had been too long since she had gotten laid. Who was she kidding? She hadn't even had a date. Her bare feet tapped out an impatient little dance of their own while one of her cats watched her warily from the doorway.

She collapsed on the edge of her single bed and squirmed a little. Those butterflies were having a blast in her stomach. She lay down and ran her fingers up her thighs, then under her skirt and inside her panties. At least she knew she could do this right. Forcibly dismissing her mental picture of Sue, she let her mind wander while her fingers played in the slick wetness beneath her skirt. No, this would be a special occasion, and dammit, she was going to get herself off to another fantasy if it killed her.

There had been a cute butch at the Film Festival last weekend. She'd do nicely. Ana remembered the woman's long fingers, imagining what they'd feel like inside her. She moaned a little, riding her own fingers. The butch's tongue would be sliding against her now, slipping inside her, then lapping up to tease her clit. Her fingertips circled it slowly, then faster. Taking her hand from her pussy, she pushed it under her shirt and pinched her nipples into small erect points, squeezing her nails into them just a bit so it would feel like teeth.

Her fantasy butch slid her fingers back inside her, one at a time. Feeling daring, she pushed one moistened finger against her asshole, barely venturing inside. It made her feel nasty and sexy, just like those fantasies that she never told Sue about. She imagined that the butch had a nice hard dildo and was working it up her ass. Grinding her hips into the bed, she rolled them in a slow sensuous circle until the heat washed from her clit up her body. Her legs stiffened and she arched her back, shuddering, frightening the cat away. She collapsed and lay still for a moment, gently grinding her hips against the patchwork coverlet.

After that, of course, there were the cats to be fed and bills to pay and all the other little errands that fill up Saturday afternoons. It still seemed like forever until they picked her up for dinner. "Don't want you chickenin' out on me," Max grumbled as she gently shoved the frantically nervous Ana out the door. Max's girlfriend Erin sat in the driver's seat of their old beater. Ana could see they were both dressed to kill. Literally. Any more studs on that leather and they'd set off metal detectors at the airport a mile away.

Erin grinned when Ana got into the car and slid her short leather jacket off her shoulder to show off her new leather bustier, laced tightly up the sides, but open enough to reveal lots of white skin. Ana oohed and aahed, all the while feeling jealous that she didn't have the nerve or the tattoos to show off like Erin did. Oh well, she thought as she settled into the back seat, they'd have to get dinner at the Cave because anywhere else Max and Erin would have the wait staff fleeing the area. Ana sat back to enjoy the ride.

Sure enough, twenty minutes later the old car pulled up outside the bar. The Cave was a dark and seedy boy bar that got turned over to the local girls once a month for the parties. The place had good sandwiches, though, which almost made up for the ambiance. Ana kept looking around curiously in the smoke filled gloom, checking out the women headed for the back room as they passed under the sickly neon beer signs. They were a pretty mixed bunch: some leatherwomen, a few butch/femme couples, lots of young, pierced goth types, but no one who really caught her eye. She turned a disappointed eye back to her turkey club. Erin made reassuring small talk until they finished eating.

"Ready?" she asked Ana gently.

"I guess," Ana took a deep breath. She didn't have to do anything she didn't want to; it would be fine. She smiled nervously at Erin and Max.

Things were just starting up when they picked up their latex and condoms at the door to the back room. The door butch sullenly pointed out the safe sex rules scrawled on the chalkboard over her head. Common sense stuff, Ana thought, breathing slowly and carefully so she wouldn't hyperventilate. She wondered if the door butch was allowed in to play. The muscular, stolid woman with her bleached flat top, tattoos and leather pants was almost her type, if Ana only had the nerve to ask.

Erin and Max towed her inside, away from temptation. The room was dark and smoky, with just enough light to see women groping each other on the benches along the sides of the room. "You want to play with us?" Max inquired, knowing the answer already. Ana shook her head and wandered over to sit on an unoccupied bench.

She watched as Max seized Erin around the waist and kissed her hard, running her hands over her black leather-covered ass. Max's hand slid lower, reaching up under the skirt and displaying Erin's fishnet stockings up to her garters. Ana could feel the wetness growing between her own legs. Surreptitiously, her hand began a slow journey up her thigh. Might as well have fun the easiest way around.

Erin and Max tossed their jackets on the bench near her, and Max pressed Erin back against the wall, arms pinned over her head. Ana watched Max's big, muscular thigh shove into Erin's crotch as Erin spread her legs in their black fishnets and spiked heels even wider to accommodate her. Glancing around, Ana noticed a couple doing a bootlicking scene in the corner. She looked away quickly. Humiliation scenes were not her thing. At least not the voluntary kind, she winced, thinking about her fights with Sue.

The three women across from her, now that was different. The women kneeling in the middle had her face buried in one woman's pussy while she took it up the ass from a hot butch wearing a harness. The three of them were moaning up a storm, and Ana's hand slid into her own pussy while she imagined that she was one of them, preferably the ones getting licked or fucked. Ooh, she was wetter than she'd been in months. Well, she'd get her money's worth anyway.

"Want some help with that?" Ana looked up to see a handsome, dark skinned butch looking down at her. She hadn't noticed this one before. From the bulge in the woman's jeans, Ana could see she was packing and tried not to purr. Must be her lucky night. How was she supposed to act? Should she ask her name first?

Wrestling with her nerves, she took a deep breath. Now or never. She took another breath to slow her pulse down and smiled invitingly at the woman. Squirming back against the bench, she slid her skirt up a little, as she slowly sucked her own juices from her fingers and watched the woman pull on her latex gloves.

The butch leaned down and pulled her to her feet as Ana strangled the "good girl" voice in her head. The woman's kiss tasted like cigarettes, beer, and peppermint gum. Ana leaned into her and wrapped her arms around her muscular neck. The butch's hand closed over her breast, covered only by a layer of red silk. Her nipples were like rocks. Her leg moved in between Ana's thighs just like Max did with Erin.

Ana just wanted to lay back on the bench and scream, "Do me now!" But maybe, she reconsidered, that wouldn't be as fun as waiting for a little while as the butch slid her hands under her short full skirt. Those big busy hands slid off her black lacy panties, slipping them slowly down her legs. Ana kicked them off, not caring if she saw them again.

Thick, sturdy fingers unbuttoned the top buttons on her blouse, then the butch lowered her mouth to Ana's hardened nipples, licking and biting them through the silk. Ana ran her fingers through her short dark hair, felt her own head tilt back as the butch ran her tongue over her neck and collarbone. She groaned as that hot mouth nibbled its way back down to her breasts.

She was leaning so far back that only the butch's strong arms were holding her up. One hand slid slowly up the outside of her thigh, then worked inward between her legs. Ana whimpered deep in her throat as the fingers slid into her soaking wet pussy. "Like that, baby?" the other woman whispered into her ear.

Ana kissed her fiercely, tongues twined, lips smashed together. She was so close to coming only her fear of falling held her back. The butch sensed this and pushed her down on the bench. Suddenly she was kneeling between Ana's legs, plastic wrap placed swiftly between her tongue and Ana's clit.

The insistent pressure of that tongue stroked up and down Ana's slit, until whole body quivering, she came with a sharp moan. "I bet you got more than that in you, don't you, honey?" she growled softly. Unzipping her jeans, she pulled out a large dildo. Ana's eyes got wide as she pulled a condom out of a nearby basket and slid it on.

Ana reached out for the woman's belt loops and pulled her forward. Slowly, sensuously, she licked her way down the dildo, then pulled it swiftly into her mouth, wondering where she got the nerve to do this. The butch's head was thrown back, one hand now burrowing into Ana's thick, dark hair, pulling her face closer, driving the dildo further into her mouth. Ana took it gladly, jerking her mouth quickly up and down the shaft.

The butch pulled suddenly out of her mouth and sat down on the bench beside her. She pulled Ana astride her lap, and slid the dildo inside her. Its long, hard length pulled a deep groan from Ana's throat as it filled her. The butch's hand slid inside her open blouse, playing with her nipples, and they kissed again. Her other hand moved over Ana's ass, then without warning, she stuck a finger up her asshole. Ana yelped into her mouth and she pulled away. "You want me to stop?" the other woman asked between gasps.

Ana shook her head and settled in to enjoy the ride. This was better than before. She could feel the other woman's finger going upward as she tightened her muscles around the dildo which was thrusting deeper and deeper inside her. She felt high, her breath coming in huge ragged gasps, so full, everything turned on at once. When she came, it was with a yell, nails raking the butch's shoulders through her shirt. Kissing her tenderly, she whispered, "What do you like, baby?"

"Do-me queens mostly," was the reply, said with a grin, and she pulled Ana up onto the bench next to her.

Glancing around, Ana saw that Erin and Max had taken over the St. Andrew's cross in the corner. Erin's bustier and net stockings were the only clothes she was still wearing and she was tied, spread eagle, to the cross. Max pulled a set of tit clamps from her pocket and fastened them to Erin's nipples, slipping them on under the supple leather. Erin's head flipped back sharply, and she moaned. Max pulled the deceptively soft leather flogger from her belt loop and ran it slowly down Erin's back and thighs.

"Hey." Ana turned swiftly back to the butch as the flogger began to snap through the air onto Erin's bare ass. "Like to watch, huh?"

Ana blushed. "Sometimes. It's not like I get the chance much. What's your name?"

"Mercedes. And yours?"

"Ana."

"Well, *dulce*, what else do you like? You want me to tie you up to that cross and whip your sweet little ass? Or maybe I'll fuck you while I make you lick off another chick." Ana's involuntary movement and faster breathing told her what she wanted to know. With one hand possessively stroking Ana's breast, rolling the nipple between her fingers, Mercedes surveyed the room. Finding what she was looking for, she beckoned to another woman.

Her fingers continued pinching and rolling Ana's nipple as they watched the other woman approach. Mercedes' fingers dragged a low moan from her throat, which made the other woman smile. She was slight and beautiful, with long black hair and a graceful, sexy walk that resembled a prowl. In her left hand, she carried a set of tit clamps that drew Ana's eyes to them in spite of herself. She imagined them tightening around her nipples. She pictured herself moaning the way Erin was, with the joy of complete surrender, and she shivered in anticipation and fear as Mercedes greeted her friend. "Ana, say hello to Yasmina."

Mercedes' other hand slid Ana's skirt up to almost, but not quite, display her pussy, while the hand playing with her nipple paused to pull her shirt open to expose her breasts. Ana gasped and writhed, and found herself spreading her legs. She looked up at Yasmina under half-closed lids and ran her tongue slowly over her lips. Suddenly she wanted these women to think that she was the hottest thing in the room. She wanted to be displayed, even owned for this one night.

Yasmina studied Ana for a long moment, gaze trailing from her red high heels up her outspread legs to the bit of dark haired pussy visible below her skirt, then over the large breasts spilling out of the red shirt. Finally she reached Ana's face and met her wide, pleading eyes. "She'll do," she concluded and reached down to tweak a nipple, then ran the cold chain connecting the clamps over her breast. "This what you're thinking about, honey?" Ana nodded, closing her eyes as the cold metal touched her tender skin. The clamp closed on her nipple. She groaned, rocking her hips as the sweet searing pain of the steel clip sent shooting heat through her, right to her cunt.

Just as suddenly, her nipple was released. Ana's eyes shot open as Yasmina slid off her baggy pants and sat next to them on the bench. "Kneel in front of her," Mercedes growled in her ear. Oh shit, what had she gotten herself into? If this woman was planning on fucking her ass with that enormous dildo, she was in trouble. The two watched her hesitation with amused smiles.

That did it. Pushing her fear down, she asked, "You got lube, right?" Her voice sounded quavery even to her.

"Don't worry, sugar. I'm going to stretch you out while you and Yasmina get acquainted," Mercedes replied with a chuckle. Ana knelt between Yasmina's lean, brown thighs and began tentatively running her tongue along them. As she moved closer, Yasmina reached down and fastened the clamps on her tits, with just enough skin so she could stand the sensation.

Ana got down on her hands and knees, trembling with excitement, ass bared for whatever Mercedes had in mind. She licked and nibbled her way up to Yasmina's clit just as the other woman stretched plastic wrap over the pussy hovering just under her questing tongue.

The first stinging slap on her round ass cheek made her jump forward instinctively. Yasmina caught her hair and ears and pulled her close, forcing her to hold the plastic with one hand. "Don't stop," she demanded. Ana's tongue pushed into the plastic as hard as she could as several more stinging slaps warmed her ass. A well-greased finger wormed its way into her asshole, just as Yasmina reached down to cup her breasts. Her hands kneaded and rubbed, tugging on the chain and the clamps, as that finger slid in and out of her ass. Ana could feel her wet juices spill out of her full pussy and run down her thighs as that finger coaxed more out of her. She stretched to open to greet it. Her tits started to burn.

A second finger followed the first into her ass, and Mercedes started to thrust into her pussy with her other hand. Yasmina tugged hard, then softly on the chain, pulling her breasts from side to side. Ana tried desperately to focus on licking her clit, reaching up with the other hand to hold the wrap in place. Soon she gave up, the other sensations overwhelming her. She came hard, shouting into Yasmina's thigh, thrusting her ass backward as her body begged for more. There were more fingers inside her now, driving her body out of control.

Groaning, supported by Yasmina's thighs, she floated in ecstasy, the unaccustomed sensations lifting her higher and higher. Suddenly, Mercedes pulled her hand from Ana's slit then her fingers from her asshole. Whimpering her disappointment, Ana started to turn in protest. Quickly, Yasmina caught her head and pulled her face back into her pussy, with a sharp tug on the chain for emphasis. Ana started licking away energetically. Mercedes smeared lube over the dildo and Ana's eager hole, then started, slowly and inexorably, to enter her. She growled softly in pain as her hole got stretched wider.

The timber of her groans and cries changed swiftly as Mercedes entered her. Yasmina's strong hands played with her breasts, sending rivers of fire through her nipples every time she touched the clamps. She came again as Mercedes began driving into her. As her thrusts got faster, Ana could feel her shaking as she came. Her ass felt as full as it could possibly get, every nerve ending blazing from her ass to her nipples. She had never felt so well and truly fucked, so thoroughly high from her orgasms that she thought she'd pass out if it went on much longer.

Sensing her exhaustion, Yasmina reached down and unfastened the clamps. The returning blood came back to her nipples with an agonizing rush as Mercedes pulled out of her ass and shoved her hand back inside her pussy. Ana was so wet and open that her whole hand fit inside as it moved swiftly in and out.

Ana came once again and collapsed at Yasmina's feet, begging for mercy. Mercedes yanked the gloves off and pulled her up onto her lap, laughing as she sat down next to Yasmina. Yasmina got up with a grin and went off to join someone else. Mercedes ran her fingers through Ana's hair and kissed her gently. "Think you'll come back next month?" Ana grinned and kissed her back, hard.

"Dunno. Maybe I'll have a girlfriend by then." She instantly regretted how wistful she sounded.

Mercedes kissed her again. "Here's my number." She handed Ana a business card. "Give me a call if you feel like it." She chucked Ana under the chin, slid her off her lap and got up. Pulling her clothes back on, she sauntered out with a quick wink back at Ana, who sat looking after with a bemused smile on her face.

What a story she'd have for Frida when she got home. The thought made her smile. She smiled even more at the card in her hand. Maybe she'd call Mercedes in a few days. But maybe it would just be enough that she could feel that Sue was gone for good. She closed her eyes, and leaning back against the wall, sat basking in the warm smell of sex from the darkened room until Max and Erin came to get her.

EMILY SAYS

Stacia can't see Emily, not even when she's lying between us at night with her fingers twisted up inside me. Not even when all I can feel is the warm pressure of her breasts against mine, her breath hot on my skin. She can't even see her when I come, when Emily's fingers and tongue pull my orgasms out of me and I jump around and moan right next to her. Stacia just goes on sleeping like she's in a coma or something while Emily laughs and laughs, licking my juices from her fingers.

It used to be Stacia's fingers inside me, her tongue in my mouth at night. I miss riding the sweaty length of her thigh, tonguing her nipples against my teeth. She doesn't disappear in the morning like Emily does. She doesn't leave me feeling exhausted and sick but so horny I don't know what I'm doing. She even used to love me. I think.

It didn't use to be like this before Emily came. I guess I was happy. But it's so hard to remember back that far, especially when Emily's around. It seems like forever even though I know that it can't have been that long. I think it's only been a month, maybe two. You know how it goes: one day you're in a relationship, bed death looming on the horizon, the next you've picked up a hot babe who takes over your life. I'm just lucky because only I can see her. At least I think that's true. Maybe Stacia's just ignoring her, waiting for the right time to dump me. I know that's what Emily would say. She says a lot of stuff like that, as long as I only want to talk about Stacia. It's a lot harder to get her to talk about herself.

Last week I asked her why Stacia couldn't see her, and she just smiled. It wasn't a happy smile, more like an *I've got a secret* smile. Then she rubbed herself against me, her thigh slick against my clit while she kissed me hard. I couldn't help myself: I kissed her back until I didn't have any more questions.

But they came back the next day when I was sitting at my desk trying not to fall asleep. At least I didn't have to call in sick. Lately I do that more and more. When Emily's not around, I can remember all the things I can't think of when she's there. Like I think I can remember meeting her at the bar. Or maybe it was at a party. I do remember that she came home with us and Stacia passed out and then it was just her and me. But Stacia can't remember any of that.

Emily says she loves me and that she'll be mine until the end. I keep meaning to ask what she means by that. I mean is it like 'till death do us part' or what? Stacia said something like that once, back before she started falling asleep right after dinner, back before I started spending a few hours on the couch with Emily every night.

I don't know much about Emily except what she likes to do in bed. But I'm not like that, not really. Last week, I even tried to get her to watch TV with me. I thought maybe we could talk. Instead, she unzipped my jeans and tore a hole in my underwear with her long red nails. Nobody ever went down on me like Emily does. When she slipped her tongue inside me, swiping its rough edge against my clit, I was all hers. But then I guess I've been all hers since she first showed up.

My clit was on fire, and I could feel the couch getting soaked underneath me the minute she touched me. She even hummed a little while she worked her fingers up inside me, like a cat purring. It feels so good when she does me, better than other any girl, better than any sex toy you can imagine. It's like she can't get enough and neither can I. She licked and licked, each swipe of her tongue, every thrust of her fingers filling me, until I bucked and heaved against her mouth. Then she laughed when I tried to moan into the pillows so Stacia wouldn't hear.

"She won't hear a thing. I promise." Then she stood up and started stripping in front of the TV, slow and sure like a pro. Once she was naked, she sat on my lap, wrapping her long legs around my waist. I was panting when she kissed me, groaning into her gorgeous breasts when she yanked my shirt and bra off. She arched her back as I worked my hand between her legs and thrust my fingers inside her. She came, or at least I think she did. Then she pulled my hand out of her and sucked on my fingers until I ached so bad that she went down on me again.

Sometimes I worry that she's not getting anything out of this, or even that she's faking it. She makes all the right noises, tastes the way she should, even smells like it's real, but I still have my doubts. But she's so beautiful, so perfect, that even her missing belly button doesn't freak me out anymore. It did at first. I mean, I'm not stupid. I know she's not like other girls I've been with. No zits, not even a mole or a wart, and she wants sex all the time. That's kind of weird, right?

I used to dream about having someone like this. Now I don't dream at all, or, if I do, I only dream about Emily. I can see her, naked and perfect every time I close my eyes. I walk around smelling of sex, wet and hot for her all day. If I go into a bathroom, I dream about her taking me up against the wall, her strong fingers covering my mouth so no one else can hear me. Sometimes, I lean against the tile walls of the bathroom at work, my fingers down my pants, rubbing and rubbing until I think my skin will come off. But I can't do it like Emily does.

I wonder what Stacia dreams about.

Emily says that Stacia's going to leave me. She's seen the signs before. First they lose interest in sex, then they lose interest in everything else. Stacia didn't even kiss me hello when I came home today. When I tried to kiss her, she said, "I'm too tired. Could you please just take a shower? How can any human being be this horny?"

I hate it when she says stuff like that. I just want to be held and touched, feel someone's naked body against mine. Someone's fingers and tongue on my skin. Stacia's just trying to make me feel bad about my needs. That's what Emily says.

I need, I need, I need it all the time. And Emily gives it to me. She comes in when I'm in the shower, washing off the cloud of lust that hangs around me ever since I met her. That's the smell that Stacia can't stand now, but I can remember when she loved the way I smelled. Or at least she said she did. Emily says that she was lying. Now Emily's bright red lips are sucking on my nipple, and she's working one finger up my ass. I'm so empty that I ache whenever she's not inside me. I crave the feel of her skin against mine, the weight of her breasts in my hands. I'd die without her, I just know I would.

I tell her that, but she just smiles. The water is cascading down on us, and I'm caressing her, trying to reach down to cup her flawless ass in my desperate hands. My body is all hers now, and I shake in her arms until they're the only thing holding me on my feet. I don't bother trying to be quiet.

Then Stacia throws the door open and just stands there looking at me. I can hear Emily laughing, but I don't think Stacia can see her. She just looks at me and shakes her head and turns away. "Stacia! Come in here with us! C'mon, baby..." I stop when I see the look on her face.

"Us? There is no 'us,' sweetie, unless you've started giving your fingers or the showerhead their own names. You're freaking me out. Finish up and let's have dinner." She turns away again, and Emily sucks harder, her sharp little teeth sinking into my nipple until I yelp. But Stacia just closes the door and doesn't look back. Whatever Stacia dreams about, it isn't me. Emily's right. She doesn't love me anymore.

The thought makes me very sad for a moment. Then Emily's mouth is sucking on my clit and her finger thrusts into my ass and I don't think anymore. At least not about anything else. She works the fingers of her other hand up inside me, and I grab at the towel rack to keep from falling over. Her fingers make a fist, stretching me wide as I can go. Pussy and ass filled all at once, and her little sandpaper tongue on my clit until I come -- shaking all over, knees giving out -- and slide down the tiles into the tub.

Emily kisses my clit tenderly and runs a finger down my jaw, almost like Stacia used to. Then she kisses me, lets me lick my own taste from her mouth. And when she's done kissing me, she jumps out of the shower and walks out the door, no towel around her or anything. I start to yell after her to put something on until I remember that Stacia can't see her anyway. Unless Stacia's lying about that too.

Emily stops in the hallway and smiles back at me with those red, red lips. Her eyes don't smile with her mouth though and it makes her look hungry and fierce. I shiver a little, but the big empty space in my pussy where her fingers live is aching again, so much that I ignore the feeling and hold my arms out to her. She blows me an air kiss and disappears down the hall.

I wonder where she goes so that I can't see her either. Maybe she lives in a different dimension where there's another version of Stacia and me. I wipe the mist off the mirror and wonder what she sees in me. I'm not beautiful like her and most of the time I just look tired. Right now I think I look sick. The skin is hanging loose off my ribs and my breasts look smaller. There are huge circles under my eyes and my skin is kind of yellow. Not surprising since I never get any sleep anymore. But that's okay because Emily loves me anyway.

I get dressed, stumbling around in a fog. When I walk into the kitchen, Stacia's waiting for me; there's some other woman I've never seen sitting at the table with her. "This is Sam," she says, like this should mean something to me. "She just dropped by for dinner."

Sam stands up and holds her hand out for me to shake. She's got short grey hair and a calm smile. She shakes my hand just right, not too short and not too long, like she's had a lot of practice at it. That's when Emily comes in. It doesn't look like Sam can see her either. She leans over the back of my chair and whispers, "Stacia brought home a shrink. She thinks you're nuts." She laughs when I glare at Stacia.

Stacia knows how I feel about shrinks, knows what they did to me when I was a kid. Once I even told her about the electroshock they used to try and make me straight. How could she do this to me? I make a huge effort and shove Emily back as gently as I can. "I'm not crazy! Just because I want sex once in awhile doesn't mean that I've got a problem! Why don't you ask Stacia why she doesn't want me anymore, doc?"

Emily starts singing in my ear so I can't hear what Sam's saying to me or what she says to Stacia. I can see their lips moving, and I think

I see Stacia wiping a tear off her cheek. I wonder what Sam said to make her cry, and I get even more pissed off. Who the hell does she think she is? Besides, it's not like Stacia would care if I really did have a problem. She just doesn't want to get blamed for it when she dumps me. That's what Emily says, and I think she's right.

I'm standing now, tears running down my cheeks, fingers tingling where they touched Emily's smoothly perfect skin. Stacia's got her hands over her face, and I can hear her crying for a minute, until Emily starts singing again. I can see Sam put her hand on Stacia's shoulder. She's looking at me, and her lips are moving, but I can't hear her very well. Emily's pressing herself against me now, grinding her breasts into my back and running her hands over my hips. I can hear Sam using words like *addiction*, but I want Emily too much to really pay attention. I imagine that if I let her do me right here on the table, they won't notice a thing and that makes me laugh. Emily laughs with me.

Stacia takes her hands away from her face and just looks at me. She looks sad and angry, and it pisses me off even more. "I've got a better girlfriend than you now! She wants me all the time!" I scream over the tune that Emily's humming in my ears. Part of me didn't want to say that. That part of me thinks that Emily's bad for me and that there's something wrong with what's going on. I imagine stomping that fear into dust, then sweeping the dust out of my head. Emily loves me. She always tells me so. Her hand slides between my legs, scorching the skin under my jeans. I rock forward against her hand, my eyes closing.

Stacia screams something, then I hear her stomping away. Sam goes with her. Emily's hand stays between my legs while her other hand works its way up my shirt and grabs my tit. I arch my back against her and she sticks her hand down inside my jeans, so loose now they don't have to be unbuttoned. I hear drawers slamming in the other room, Stacia sobbing and cursing, Sam saying something quiet.

But Emily's hand is inside me and I don't need anything else. Not Stacia or sleep or food. I can just live on love. I start laughing as the front door slams and Emily rubs my clit just right. My knees are too weak to hold me up, and I fall on the floor, but Emily catches me before I hit the tiles. She unbuttons my pants and drops those red lips to my slit, and I come and I come and I come until I can't move anymore. I ask her to stop and she laughs and she looks for a new way to make my body sing in her hands. I wonder if Stacia could even see me now. Then Emily says she'll stay with me to the end, and I smile at her as I fade away, my hips bucking to the pressure of her tongue.

The Hands of a Princess

Commander Agnes Helensdottir, known as 'Agnes the Bloody' to her foes, stared at the ground between her feet and sighed. It was a deep sigh, one that shook the tent around her and it was enough to make her swordsister, Eriel One-Eye, open her remaining orb and glare at her. Eriel was an excellent shot with a throwing knife, even after she'd drained her cups like she had last night. Agnes vowed that she would sigh no more and exhaled deeply and wistfully with the thought. Instinct alone made her duck to one side and let the mug that Eriel hurled in the direction of her head shatter on the trunk behind her.

"What in the Seventeen Hells is your problem? You won't lie with Rosie even when the wench throws herself at you, you don't joke when you drink and you wouldn't even fight those bastards from Drey's Sworn last night. We had to avenge your honor without you, not that the Sworn stayed for much avenging." Eriel sat up with this explosion of words and gripped her head in her hands.

Silently, Agnes extended a mug of the slop that the company's cook gave them each morning. Eriel seized it and chugged it down, finishing it off with a choked cough. "Fool's trying to kill us, I swear."

"I don't know, Eriel. I just want something more than this." An expansive wave took in the weather-beaten field tent. "Do you ever wonder what it would like to...I don't know...not fight all the time?"

"On your feet, ladies." The General's Second threw back the tent flap and ducked inside. Agnes stifled a yawn but neither woman obliged him by leaping to her feet. "General's orders. We got a new assignment for you two." He leered in a way that made Eriel reach for one of her knives. He stopped leering.

"What's the General want, Harold? Yeah, I know I'm not supposed to call you that." Eriel stretched with a weary sigh of her own and gave their visitor a sneer.

"You'll need to report to the Palace today. Princess Berenara is leaving tomorrow to go to Virain to wed Prince Keral and the King wants to make sure she's well guarded on the journey. Prince Deren is taking his rejection hard, says he'll have the princess at any cost. King Tedore asked for you two special, gods alone know why." He shrugged as if to signify his contempt.

"Because we're war heroes with more medals than you can count, you fool," Agnes growled. In truth, the General's Second could not be farther from her thoughts. A chance to ride at the Princess' side! Here at last was her chance to find out if the beautiful Berenara shared her mother's fondness for well-muscled female warriors.

The Swordsisters' barracks in town rang with tales of Queen Amadia's conquests. Clothilde Battlespawn even claimed that she couldn't ride for a week afterward. Agnes would have traded places with her in a heartbeat, but somehow she was always on the battlefield or on duty when the Queen required companionship. Besides, how did you attract the notice of a Queen so that she wanted to…do things to you? She sighed again.

Harold realized he was being ignored and finally stalked out, leaving them to their morning toilette. Agnes stopped sighing. Now was the time for hot baths and polishing their armor and swords until they glowed. Even the battle tattoos on her hands and arms looked polished when she was done. They reported to the palace with time to spare despite Eriel's protests. "C'mon Aggie, just one last trip to the Salted Cod. They're not expecting us for hours yet. I'm as dry as--"

"Their Majesties will see you now." The gatekeeper raised her eyebrows in surprise but let them in to follow the footman. Agnes straightened her back and thrust out her already impressive chest, strutting so her blade swung at her side. Several medals gleamed on her breastplate and she polished them surreptitiously with her leather sleeve when she thought Eriel wouldn't notice.

King Tedore was, unlike his wife and daughter, golden-haired, virile and eminently forgettable. His eyes glowed with wisdom and benevolence and he greeted them with a kindly smile, one that gave them leave to look at the rest of the royal family. Today that consisted solely of Princess Berenara. She favored her mother's dark good looks, coupled with a body that looked like it would be unbearably sweet to hold and brown eyes sparkling with sardonic humor and intelligence. Not classically beautiful to be sure, but you noticed her when you came into the room.

Agnes swept off her helmet in her best bow. "You sent for us, your Majesty?" She made herself look at the King, not the Princess. There would be no thinking about how the latter would feel in her arms. There would be no sweet dreams about any arbitrary and capricious punishments that lady might dream up in the middle of the night. Not a one. She could feel a rosy blush heat her ears but managed not to curse.

King Tedore was oblivious as he outlined their mission but Agnes could see Berenara smiling from the corner of her eye and it made her blush even more. It was fortunate that Eriel had come with her because she heard almost none of the King's commands. The Princess had lovely big hands, all long fingers and broad palms. At least they were lovely for what Agnes was thinking about. The blush spread over her cheeks as she felt a hot stab of pure lust between her legs.

After that, no stern internal warnings would serve. Eriel had to tow her away from the throne room where the marvelously desirable princess seemed to be smothering a laugh. "Do you want to get us locked up in the dungeons, you idiot? She's not one of your tavern wenches!"

Agnes stumbled as Eriel yanked her by the arm. "I know! I'm not a fool! Now let go of me before I stick my dagger in your belly," Agnes snarled, one meaty hand finding the hilt in her belt.

"All right, just so as you remember that tomorrow. Now I'm for the Salted Cod. You coming?"

Agnes mumbled something inaudible as she walked away, glowering in a manner that she hoped looked purposeful. Not that she had anything to do except polish her armor and daydream, but it would do. Then she only had to pass a sleepless night listening to Eriel's snores and imagining Berenara doing things to her that no real Princess was likely to contemplate. Dawn came far too early.

Still, they managed to stumble along to the palace in good order to join up with the rest of the Princess' entourage. Agnes and Eriel rode next to the Princess's carriage as befitted an honor guard and did their best to look the part. At least they gave her Highness' maids something to giggle about; Eriel had ample opportunity for rolling her single eye.

Despite the honor, Agnes did find herself wondering why the Princess seemed to have so many servants and so few guards for this journey. It was hard not to remember Harold's words, "Prince Deren says he'll have her at any cost." The thought made her watch the trees and fields on either side of the King's Road for signs of trouble. When they made camp for the night, she circled the area carefully, making sure that the few sentries were awake and at their posts.

She had no sooner resolved to take up sentry duty herself when, much to her surprised delight, the Princess sent for her. She went to the Royal Tent with a pounding heart and a newly awakened aching between her legs that she didn't think could ever be satisfied. It only got worse when she entered with a sweeping bow to find Berenara lying face down on her bed, barely covered with a fine silk sheet. "The Princess requests that you sooth her aches and pains with the warrior's touch," the simpering maid informed Agnes. From the way that she ran her fingers over Agnes' well-muscled forearm, she wouldn't have minded a little touching herself.

Not that Agnes noticed. The warrior's touch! Surely she wasn't good enough to lay hands on a princess. She stammered out something to that effect only to have the maid tug at the straps holding her armor in place. "You can't wear all this and massage the Princess. You might hurt her." The maid got close enough that Agnes could feel her breasts brush against her back as she pulled her armor off.

This even Agnes, besotted as she was, could not fail to notice. Especially since Berenara chose that moment to turn her head and watch them. "Let her be, Mira. I hurt all over from bouncing around in the carriage all day. I'm told you have the best hands in the regiment, Commander and I truly have need of them tonight." The Princess stretched beneath her silk coverings so that they slid down, baring the lovely pale skin of her back.

Agnes bit back a whimper and forgot her worries about the sentries. The maid gave her a saucy smile, contriving to pinch Agnes' buttock with one hand as she gestured with the other toward the oils and the scents that waited on the table next to the Princess' bed. Then she blew the warrior a kiss and vanished from the tent, leaving Agnes alone with Berenara. The warrior could scarcely believe her good fortune. She bounded eagerly to the Princess' side and took a deep breath to still her trembling hands. "I'll do my best, your Highness." Berenara's full lips curved in a small smile and she wiggled against the bed in what could only be anticipation.

Agnes poured a bit of oil on her hands and rubbed them together, savoring the moment before she touched that creamy skin. This would only be the beginning. Surely Berenara could be persuaded to use those hands of hers in all the ways that Agnes longed to be touched; she was her mother's daughter after all. Giddy with anticipation, she lowered her hands to the Princess' shoulders and rubbed gently. "Harder," Berenara commanded. Agnes ventured to brace one knee on the bed and to dig her fingers in a bit deeper. Berenara inched closer so that one of her well-padded hips rested against Agnes' knee.

For the first time in her life, Agnes understood swooning. The tent disappeared around her until all she could see was the woman on the bed. The sheet slipped lower as the Princess squirmed then fell off entirely as she stretched up to reach for her goblet on the table. One sweet round breast was clearly visible and the warrior had to force herself not to reach for it. "Would you like some wine, Commander? I know this is an unworthy task for such a brave hero but everything just aches so much." She gave Agnes a bewitching smile over one shoulder then laid down again.

"No thank you, Highness. It...it is an honor to serve you," Agnes choked out the words as she tried to pretend that she was merely massaging one of her swordsisters. But the lack of prominent scars, among other things, made that impossible. Her thighs were wet now and she ached with desire, something she had never felt for any of her swordsworn.

"That's not where it hurts most, Commander." The Princess reached back and slipped one of Agnes' hands down to the top of her thigh, just below her splendid bottom. "Right around there. Don't be afraid to really get in there, Commander. You have a wonderful touch. I'm feeling better already." She squirmed a little so that Agnes' fingers slipped between her thighs. "Oooh, yes. That aches so much."

Scarcely believing her good fortune, Agnes grabbed for the oil with her free hand and poured far too much on the Princess' rounded buttocks and soft creamy thighs. Then she scrambled to rub it in before Berenara noticed, rubbing her hands over and between the Princess' thighs in a way she had feared impossible the night before. Berenara moaned happily and spread her legs so that Agnes' thumb found its inadvertent way into her very wet slit. The warrior froze until the Princess wriggled down a bit further, just enough so that Agnes' finger disappeared inside her.

What else may have occurred then had they not been interrupted will never be known. Suddenly, shouts and the clash of steel rang from outside the tent. Eriel charged in, blade drawn. "We're under attack! The sentries were overpowered and we need your sword!"

Cursing, Agnes flung the sheet back over the started Princess and dove for her sword. Eriel ran out, muttering an apology. Agnes was on her heels, sword in hand as she emerged to come face to face with a member of Drey's Sworn Company. "Have you turned traitor then? You shall feel my steel draining your life away this night, scum!"

"Stop your babble and kill him already!" Eriel bellowed. She attempted to suit her actions to her words and slashed at her opponent, wounding his thigh so that he fell back. Agnes beat down her own opponent's attack with a few well-placed blows, then feinted right. A quick twist of her wrist drove her blade into his shoulder She spun, jerking the blade lose with a single swift motion and countered an attack from another of Drey's men. Soon, she and Eriel were back to back, hewing their way through their attackers as they came on in seemingly endless waves.

But even their prowess was not enough. Eriel slipped in the carnage around her and took a wound to her arm when her blade got stuck in a fallen enemy. She scrambled to her feet but not before one of her opponents managed to slice Agnes' arm. Agnes uttered a battle cry loud enough to strike terror into the heart of any foe and switched her sword to her right hand. It entered the man's side like it was butter and he fell with a gurgled scream. Three more fell under their blades before they were overrun by sheer numbers and found themselves surrounded.

The man who led their attackers rode up behind them. "Bravely fought. Tedore chose well when he selected you. I don't suppose you'd entertain a better offer?" The expression in Prince Deren's cold gray eyes made him seem far older than his actual years.

He rode his horse well, Agnes noted dispassionately, sitting the saddle with a warrior's grace. She measured her distance from him, calculating how many men she'd have to cut down in order to reach him. Too many, too far. Besides, he could always ride away. How would she save her princess now? She schooled her face not to show her thoughts and tried instead to listen to what Eriel was saying.

"And what would King Tedore's cousin and heir want with such insignificant soldiers as ourselves?" Eriel's voice was silky, dangerous. She too must have measured the ground between them.

"Yes, I'd like to hear that as well." Princess Berenara flung aside the closed flap of her tent and emerged fully dressed. Agnes noted this with some regret.

Deren swept a bow from his horse and dismounted with style. Berenara responded by crossing her arms over her bosom and raising an eyebrow. "Your Highness is as lovely as ever. I do regret any inconvenience that my actions tonight may have caused. My men have perhaps been overzealous."

Agnes took in the ring of armed men surrounding them and snorted loudly. Berenara's full lips twisted in the tiniest of smiles but she did not take her eyes from Deren's face. "Am I your prisoner, cousin?"

"My wife to be, fairest flower. Treated with all the honor and respect due to your position, of course." Deren's voice was polite, conciliatory but the blades hemming Agnes and Eriel in did not waver.

Berenara's gaze swept over them but her expression did not change as she met the Prince's false smile. "Indeed. Then perhaps your men would release my guards. Surely you would not want to bring your betrothed to the capital escorted only by your men." One delicate foot tapped impatiently on the dirt beneath it.

"Certainly my love. As soon as they relinquish their swords. I would not have it said that I cannot protect my bride."

Agnes met Berenara's eyes over the heads of the armsmen, pleading for permission to cut her way through the armored obstacles before her. If she moved at full battle speed, she might be able to slay enough of them that her princess could flee to the woods. It was not to be; she could read as much in those beautiful dark eyes and it pained her as much as the wounds she was trying to ignore.

But the Princess' next words surprised her as much as they seemed to startle Deren. "Let us not entertain your armsmen with our discourse, Highness. If you would accompany me I have a fine vintage in my tent. We can discuss our arrangements in comfort." Berenara fluttered her eyelashes at the Prince and Agnes' gut twisted with pure jealousy. "Provided of course that my guards are posted outside. With their swords drawn. And my wounded soldiers are attended to."

"Ah, my flower—"

"These are my terms, cousin. Now surely you'd like to see the inside of my tent?" She gave him an arch smile and Agnes' spirits plummeted.

Prince Deren nodded reluctantly as though his head were on strings. "Tend to the wounded. Let these two go to their posts but watch them," he muttered to his commander as he followed Berenara's swaying hips into the Royal Tent. Agnes and Eriel limped after him and took up position on either side of the closed flap. Their opponents followed them, standing in a loose semi circle around them with swords drawn. In truth, the tent was probably the safest place in the land for that hour.

Agnes rubbed her thumb and tried not to weep with frustration. To have been so close to feeling those hands driving her to unimaginable bliss and to fail: it was too much. If only she had…asked. Begged. Groveled. But she had never asked for anything before, let alone begged.

The Princess giggled in the tent behind them and Deren gave an odd sounding grunt. Agnes clenched her jaw tightly.

"How's the arm?" Eriel muttered as if the armsmen a few feet away couldn't hear them.

"Fine. Like these pigstickers could hit a cow with those iron bars they've been waving around." Agnes glared at their guards. They glared back and everyone settled in for a long standoff, serenaded by strange noises from the tent.

Dawn was brightening the sky when Prince Deren finally emerged, moving slowly and carefully. He kissed Berenara's hand with a cautious grace. "Until tomorrow, dear lady." She gave him a charming smile as he swung stiffly up onto his horse and ordered his men to follow. He turned toward the road, pausing only to add a curt "Release them." With a clatter of hooves and the clank of armor, his men followed him out of the camp, each face wearing a different shade of stunned surprise. Behind them that same expression was echoed on the faces of Berenara's men, Agnes and Eriel.

"What did you do?" Agnes demanded, then amended it to "What did you say to him, Highness?" at Eriel's glare.

"Averted a civil war, of course. My cousin has agreed to my terms and we will wed in a few months time. Neither of us will interfere with the pleasures of the other, provided an heir is born. Father didn't think I could manage it but Mother told me everything I needed to know." Berenara stretched and yawned.

"And Prince Keral?" Agnes could not stop the words. Her mind reeled. Her thighs trembled. Her princess was capable of anything.

"Is a good natured fool. I never intended to go to Virain, I'm afraid. Marrying Deren will make it far easier to keep an eye on him. Now onto more important matters. Are either of you wounded badly?"

Eriel shrugged and a sluggish stream of blood ran down her arm. The Princess raised an eyebrow and beckoned a servant to her side. "Have their wounds tended to. My apologies, Captain, Commander. We appreciate your loyalty and will reward it well." Her glance took in both of them and Agnes' stomach did a slow leisurely flip. "Get some sleep."

With that, the Princess turned to walk toward the tent, then stopped to glance over her shoulder at Agnes. "Commander, why don't you come back when your wounds are bandaged? I'd like to have you work on my aches and pains a little more if you don't mind." Her full lips curved in a smile that almost brought Agnes to her knees. She nearly staggered into the tent behind those bewitching hips and was only prevented from doing so by the servant who was trying to clean her wound.

Moments later, she bolted for the Royal Tent as though possessed. Somewhere behind her, she could hear Eriel laughing. But once she stood before the Princess, she was too flustered to speak for a long moment. Berenara merely sat on the bed and looked puzzled and expectant. It was that look that finally loosened Agnes' tongue. How did you grovel anyway? She wasn't sure but clearly she needed to ask for what she wanted.

"I failed to protect you, Highness," she muttered into her armored chest. "I should be punished." The thought of Berenara's hands on her bare flesh was almost more than she could bear and the ache between her legs changed to a throb. No, it was too much. She couldn't bring herself to look up and meet the merry eyes that searched her face.

A silence followed. "Indeed, Commander. And what punishment would you choose?" Berenara rose and walked over to stand in front of Agnes. She reached out and forced the warrior's chin upwards until their eyes met. The breath caught in Agnes' throat so that she could not speak and she was left to stare longingly into those dark eyes. Berenara pulled her face down for a long kiss, drinking from her lips as though from a flagon. Agnes' knees began to buckle even as her arms went cautiously around the Princess' waist.

"How dare you touch me without my express permission?" Agnes jerked her hands away. "That's better. But not quite good enough,

Commander. I think I may be able to think of a suitable punishment for you after all." She beckoned Agnes forward and the warrior walked to her on quivering thighs. "Strip." Those lips curled in a smile that made Agnes' juices run hot down her legs.

Clumsily, she tugged at her leather shift and her remaining garments until she had shed them all and stood trembling before the Princess. Berenara walked slowly around her, studying her scars and battle tattoos until Agnes' ears turned a lovely shade of scarlet. She trailed one finger up the warrior's back until Agnes' skin stood out all over with goosebumps. "Kneel here," she commanded, gesturing to the floor next to the bed.

Agnes hastened to obey, glad to be able to kneel before her legs failed her. "This," said Berenara as one of her long fingered hands met the flesh of Agnes' buttock with a resounding smack, "is for making me stay awake and attending to your needs rather than the other way around." A second smack followed the first, then a third. Agnes' thighs ran wet and trembled beneath her. She reached out to brace herself against the bed.

"Oh, we can't have that." Berenara reached into a trunk and pulled out several silk scarves. "Lie on the bed." Agnes writhed up onto the silken sheets, breathless with anticipation. Berenara bound each of her limbs to the bed with an easy speed that suggested some practice. Agnes wriggled happily, her desire pooling beneath her until the silken covers were soaked.

Each of Berenara's slaps seemed to echo through the aching emptiness between her legs and she began to beg to feel the Princess' hands inside her. This, then was what surrender felt like: to be helpless before the whims of another, to make her body yield to their desires. She ached for more, overwhelmed with longing to feel her princess' hands inside her, filling her.

At first, she only whispered her desires, soft sounds barely audible over the harshness of their breathing, the sound of flesh on flesh. She could never face Eriel again if she knew about this. Could she? Then as the force of Berenara's blows drove her farther from herself, she moaned, she howled her longing into the emptiness, no longer caring if the entire camp heard the Swordsister conquered by need.

But Berenara was relentless. When her hand tired, she pulled out a small flat paddle that seemed to have been made for the purpose and applied it with zeal. Agnes yielded further, bellowing submission even as she reveled in it.

Finally those long fingers, those clever and capable hands, slid inside her, filling her until they were all she could feel. They slid deeper and deeper on the river of her juices and she strained against the bed, trying to take in the Princess' entire hand. Her hips rocked up and back with an energy she'd never felt off the battlefield. Let Berenara only see how eager she was, how completely hers she would become and all would be well. She convulsed around those fingers with that fervent hope, back arched against her bonds and shouting her release into the silken pillows.

"You're much more fun than any of the others." The Princess smiled mischievously as she shed her dress to lay down on top of Agnes. The warrior moaned happily as her bonds were loosened and she rolled over to take Berenara in her arms. "Let's see what else you can do." Agnes slipped down between her legs to plant a kiss on her lady's bare flesh. She lapped her juices, drinking them in with a savage desire that soon had Berenara flaying against the bed, her moans ringing out. And Eriel would be happy that there would be no more sighing, she thought as she worked her own fingers inside her princess.

ANONYMOUS

"Wht r u wearing?" It was so corny I had to laugh before I looked to see who sent it. I thought about answering it even if I'd gotten it by mistake. Like I had the nerve. I smiled and checked the send address; it didn't look familiar so I deleted it from my phone and forgot about it.

At least until the second one a few hours later. "Wht r u wearing?" I was still at work and it wasn't going so well. I'd be seeing overtime for sure tonight and probably this weekend, quite a few hours of it at this rate. The same thing that made me laugh this morning was pissing me off this afternoon. I answered the message. "Wht do u care? Go away!" I clicked Send, glad for a minute that I could take my rotten day out on someone else, especially when they deserved it. Perv.

I thought about turning my phone off but then my soon-to-be-divorced sister Cara and the West Coast office couldn't get in touch with me and we couldn't have that. I sighed at the thought. Sure enough, my phone rang again just then. I checked the number to be on the safe side, and this time I grinned. That's what best friends are for, right? "Hey, Gerry, what's up?"

What was up was that she wanted to go out tonight to check out the new women's night at one of the boy bars. And as usual, I was going to have to be the voice of reason. "On a Wednesday? You gotta be kidding me. Besides, I have to work tonight. You still think we're twenty-three or

94

something?" She giggled and wouldn't let me off the phone until I agreed to go next week, which I did with my usual eye roll. It wasn't like we'd meet anyone there anyway. Well, she would. There was a lot to be said for being cute and bubbly.

Great. Now I could spend the rest of the day whining to myself about my looks and personality and why I was still single, two years after Amy and I broke up. The day was just getting better and better.

I slogged through it though and went home eventually. I had just fed the cats and collapsed in front of the TV with warmed up leftovers when the phone buzzed again. I picked it up, figuring it'd be Gerry but no, I couldn't get that lucky. "Wht r u wearing?" This was one persistent perv, I had to give them that.

I turned off the phone. To hell with the West Coast office and needy siblings alike. I crashed soon afterwards and managed not to have a single dream about much of anything, at least not that I could remember.

The next morning was nondescript until I turned my phone back on. There were a couple of messages: one from my sister Cara, one from Gerry and one from an address I didn't recognize. My heart thumped a little faster on that one so I decided to open it first and get it over with. There it was: "I bet it's ht!," complete with a little heart.

This time, I just stared at it for a few minutes. What the hell was going on? I didn't give my number or email address out much, and I couldn't imagine anyone I knew sending me these things. Which meant that this was coming from someone I didn't know, at least not well. The thought made me queasy and hot all at once.

The messages could be coming from some nut case. On the other hand, they could be from someone who had a crush on me. Or who maybe just got off on sending text messages to strangers. Then I could be anyone, even a smoking hot gal who spent her workday text messaging her lover. I weighed the options. It was just imaginary sex anyway, not like meeting someone for real, warts and all. Why not?

I answered the message this time: "I'm nt wearing a thng. U?"

I giggled for a good minute after I sent it since it was 9 AM and anyone who knew me knew how unlikely it was that I was either late to work or at my desk naked. Then I dealt with Cara and my boss for while, saving Gerry for later. I wondered if I should tell her about my new admirer, but I decided against it. She'd just laugh at me and tell me I needed a real girlfriend.

Then the West Coast office called and my day was off and running. I almost forgot about my text message buddy until Gerry called again just before 5. We made dinner plans and I finished up what I was working on, then packed up the work I had to take home and got ready to go. My phone vibrated and I picked it up, half expecting it to be Cara again.

Instead, I got a woman's voice I didn't recognize on the other end. "Really? I'd like to see that. I'm just wearing my panties and they're soaking wet cause I'm thinking about you." The voice purred into my ear like a lover's tongue or what I could remember of that sensation. Then, while I was staring at my phone in complete disbelief, the caller clicked off.

I fumbled with the phone for a minute, then checked to see where the call had come from. With shaking fingers, I called the number back only to get the answering machine for some dry cleaners on the other side of town. What the hell was going on?

I wasn't getting any answers but I had to admit that part of me was liking this. And judging from the way I was feeling, liking it a little too much. I wondered if my pervy secret admirer was cute and spent a fun couple of minutes remembering a woman I'd seen at one of the local coffeeshops. But by the time I'd given her Angelina Jolie's lips, I had to head home, weird admirers or no weird admirers.

I didn't hear from my mystery caller again that day. Or the next. By then, I'd decided that it was all probably a mistake. Maybe she thought I was someone else. I took myself out for a mocha latte on Saturday morning. That, of course, was my phone buzzed again. I picked it up and grinned a little to myself when I saw the text message waiting for me. "I'd <heart> to kiss u all over." Still corny. I found myself looking around and getting just a bit wet wondering if she was somewhere nearby.

But if she was I couldn't tell. I thought about her while I ran errands and went jogging. Thought about her even more when I was trying to get work done. I pictured her holding the vibrator I had pressed to my clit about fifteen minutes later. And the dildo I had shoved up inside me a few moments after that. I bucked and rolled against all that sensation, all that imaginary skill until I came hard once from the pressure, then again from picturing her watching me. Not quite enough but fun anyway.

I had just collapsed all sweaty and breathless on my pillows when the phone rang again. I grabbed it with sticky fingers and fumbled to get the message to display. "Come to ur windw. The 1 by the firescape." There was no way. She must not know me or she'd realize that I live in a second floor apartment that's about four feet away from the one across the alley. Hanging out naked in front of it meant I'd be advertising myself as the neighborhood slut.

I typed "No" and sent the message. It made me feel a little sad and empty, like I'd had a chance to do something really crazy and fun and turned it down. Then I realized that she had to be somewhere nearby if she could see my bedroom window. I wondered if I could see her. I got up and tiptoed over to hide behind the curtains and peak around them out at the fire escape and the alley below. Nothing. I checked out the apartment windows across the way but most of them had their blinds pulled so I couldn't see anything.

That was when the phone buzzed again. This time instead of the heart, there was a sad little face. I couldn't keep myself from laughing. That made it all even sillier somehow and I jumped out from behind the curtain, then jumped back. I figured it was sort of like flashing. I glanced down at the phone. This time the message said: "I'd luv to wtch u ply w urslf."

I'll bet she would. This was going way too far. It was bad enough that this woman knew where I lived. I was not putting on a show for some nut I didn't even know. I hung up and got dressed instead, this time feeling like I was making the right choice. Armed with a sense of self-righteousness, I got to back to work and managed to make some progress.

Or at least enough so that I could justify going out with Gerry on a Saturday night. She was at her best and busy being a blast to hang out with, the way she was when she had a new romance. But if she had a new girlfriend, she hadn't mentioned her to me. I decided not to ask so I could be all surprised when I met the latest squeeze. Not that they ever seemed to be around that long. Gerry's track record was worse than mine, at least to me. I'd managed to stay with Amy for three whole years after all.

Pity I couldn't hang that on a sign around my neck along with "Shows real staying power!" No one was giving me a second glance except when they had to be polite enough to look away from Gerry. I sulked into my gin and tonic and thought about finding myself a friend who made me look cuter instead of invisible.

But it wasn't like it was her fault. She was blonde, stacked and had a smile that could light up a room. She was also smart and funny, which was why I hung out with her and had since college. Tonight she was needling me in between invitations to dance and strangers buying her drinks. "You've gotta take some chances, you know. If you don't put yourself out there, nothing's going to happen." And so on. Same pep talk she'd been giving me for a year ever since it became obvious that I wasn't just going to bounce back from my last breakup.

This time instead of actually listening, I zoned out and thought about my mystery fan. I wondered what would have happened if I had walked up the window and maybe cupped my naked boobs, running my thumbs over them until they were really sensitive.

Then I could've run my hands slowly down my body like I was the hottest thing around, maybe done some cool and weird thing that hadn't occurred to me yet before I started rubbing my clit. Maybe I'd have stuck my fingers inside my pussy then brought them up to my mouth and licked them off one by one. Or, if I backed things up a little, maybe I would've gone to the window still wearing my blouse. Then I could've unbuttoned it very, very slowly while I caressed my clit.

"Hey, what're you grinning about?" Gerry snapped her fingers under my nose. "You got some kind of imaginary date thing going on in there?"

I jumped a little and stared back at her. Her blue eyes were at their most innocent: big deep pools that screamed "I'm not up to anything!" A horrible thought struck me. What if my caller was some buddy of hers who she'd put up to calling me? Someone who was only calling me so that she'd sleep with them out of gratitude? I got seriously depressed, enough so that I almost started crying. That was it; I told Gerry I wasn't feeling good and told her I'd catch a cab home but she insisted on driving me home anyway.

Then she insisted on coming up to make sure I was okay. No amount of telling her that I was just feeling sick seemed to do the trick. But there was no way I was going to tell her about my unknown friend now, not when there was a chance that it was all about pity. There were just some depths I wasn't willing to sink to. At least not for an active fantasy life.

She finally took off after tucking me with a warm milk laced with something she found in the kitchen, so at least I knew that I still had the coolest best friend around. As I dozed off, I caught myself wondering what it would be like to be with her. Then I woke up the next morning from a vivid dream about having to fight my way through crowds of women to get near her.

Besides, sleeping with your best friend was a really bad idea. I'd learned that in our college baby dyke years and sworn off it back then. I realized I must really be down if I was thinking of making a play for Gerry and I decided that I was going to dedicate the day to pulling myself out of it. I dragged myself out of bed and showered, then called a friend for lunch. I had coffee and did some odds and ends around the apartment, then met my lunch date. Then I took myself out shopping. By the end of the day I was feeling better and even had enough energy to call Cara back and make sympathetic noises.

By the time I'd finished my next round of overtime work, I was almost glad to hear my phone ring. At least it meant I had a life of sorts, even a mostly imaginary one. Sure enough, it was my mystery woman. "I'm thnkng abt the wy u tste." That one was enough to send a hot flash from my pussy to every nerve ending in the rest of my body. And get me thinking about the way she might taste too, for that matter.

I stopped to think about what to say next. No point in this being completely one sided after all. "Wsh yr tngue ws in me nw." No hearts, no smiley faces. Somehow they didn't quite capture what I was thinking about.

I wondered if she'd want to meet for coffee or something, but only for a second until I gave myself a good solid forehead slap. The whole point of this thing, as far as I was concerned, was that I didn't know who this was. If that changed, it would get weird and complicated and we'd break up because she was sleeping with someone else or because I spent too much time at work. I'd been down the relationship path before and I wasn't getting burned again.

Besides, my hand was between my legs now and my fantasy lover was getting me hotter and wetter than I'd been the whole last six months with Amy. I rubbed and stroked, letting my fingers send shocks through my clit until I came sitting at my desk. I had never done that before and it made me wonder if I could get away with it at work.

All of it was almost enough to make me ignore my phone. But not quite. I picked it up and got my mystery woman on the other line. "Come to the window this time. Please." Her voice was breathy and hot, like she'd been running. Or like her own hand had been doing some exploring.

I got up and walked over to the window. This time I thought I could see one of the blinds across the way open a little. Not enough so that I could see in but enough so that I knew I was being watched. Where it came from, I have no idea, but suddenly I wanted to be wanted. I wanted someone to go nuts wanting to touch me. Even if it was someone I didn't know and might never know. Gerry's gratitude fuck, if that's who this was, was going to have something else to think about.

I decided to put on a show. I walked over to the closet and pulled off the t-shirt and jeans I was wearing. Then I pulled off the bra and put on the silkiest button-down shirt I owned. I took off my panties and pulled on a loose-fitting pair of dress slacks on instead. The soft fabrics felt cool against my bare skin and I felt like I was getting away with something. I glanced at myself in the mirror and thought *Yeah, Wild Thing. That's me.*

But it was enough to give me the courage for the next thing I wanted to do. I picked up the phone and text messaged: "U wtchng?"

I got a smiley face in answer and I strutted over to the window in the dressiest shoes I could dig out of the closet. Sure, my balance wasn't terrific in them but they looked great and right now that was all they needed to do.

I put on some music, whatever was closest to hand and seemed raunchiest. I think I ended up with 'Bolero' but by then it didn't really matter all that much. I took a deep breath and looked across the alleyway. The blind was still open and I thought I could see some fingers holding it down. Just to be on the safe side, I glanced at the other windows. It didn't look like anyone else was home.

Hoping for the best, I pulled the blind up. Then I kissed the phone and put it down on the windowsill. I reached up to the top button on my blouse and I started unbuttoning it. Just the first two for starters. I ran my hands up my thighs and waist and cupped my breasts in my hands, like I'd imagined myself doing earlier. The music was getting to me now, filling me enough that I was willing to roll my hips with it. I reached down and ran my finger along the damp center seam of my pants. They were getting soaked as I got into it and I grinned a little.

I wondered how my audience was feeling and I unbuttoned a couple more buttons. I leaned forward so that she could see all the cleavage I had and rolled my shoulders a little like I'd seen some woman do at a burlesque show that Gerry dragged me to.

That gave me another idea. I reached over into my dresser drawer and pulled out a long silky scarf that I almost never wore. Then I put it between my legs, an end in each hand, and pulled it back and forth nice and slow. Once I was so hot I nearly came from that alone, I pulled it out and held it tight over my boobs. I unbuttoned the last couple of buttons and pulled the shirt open under the scarf. You could see my nipples a mile away through the sheer fabric and I wondered how my audience was liking the view.

I looked out at the window across the way and the hand holding the blind reached out and gave me a thumb's up. I grinned and unbuttoned the dress slacks. I thought about taking them off but then I decided not to give the whole show away. Not just yet. I slipped the blouse off and tied the scarf around me. You could still see my boobs through it but not too clearly. Then I slipped my right hand down my pants and found my clit.

I danced around while I rubbed it, rolling my hips for emphasis. When my fingers were good and wet, I pulled them out of my crotch and licked them off slowly, sticking each finger in my mouth and tasting myself like I was an ice cream cone.

Then I stuck one hand back into my pants and reached up with the other to twist my nipples just a little through the scarf. I got the pressure on my clit just right and I managed to come standing up, though I had to let go of my tit to grab the window to make sure I didn't fall over. It was one of those deep orgasms, the kind that make your whole body shake and make you go weak at the knees before they're done with you.

I collapsed on the bed before I was quite finished, even though I knew she couldn't see me there. Some things are best left to the imagination. The aftershocks swept me away for a few minutes and I rode them out until I was sated.

That was when the phone rang again. I picked it up and saw a text message that read: "Sme tme nxt Sunday???"

What else could I say? "Sure." With a little smiley face this time. I pulled the blinds down and stood there for a minute, wondering if I'd tell Gerry about this now. I was pretty sure I wouldn't, at least not yet. But that meant I was still at the window when I saw someone leave the building across the way. She was wearing a jacket and a hat and I only saw her from the back but she looked familiar. I thought about calling her, seeing if I could get her to turn around so I could get a look at her face.

But I decided against it. Sometimes not knowing is the best part.

THE OLD SPIES CLUB

The message said to meet Gia at the café just off the main plaza at nine but I showed up early, just because. Old habits die hard. I took mental notes on what I might need without too much effort. At least I wasn't getting that rusty in my old age. First, the escape routes: one back door and the plaza itself, filled with evening crowds. Check. Then the potential weapons: one electrical line running over the tables that could be pulled down if necessary. The chairs were mostly wood and fragile enough to break on impact but sturdy enough to be used as clubs in a pinch. There were a few other things that might work if I needed them. It would do.

I curled up in a doorway across the square to watch the place for a while. To pass the time, I thought about the last time I'd seen Gia. It had been years ago, just before I left for South America and she headed out to Kashmir. We'd met in a café like this one. She'd brought a gun, of course but I hadn't had much trouble taking it away from her. Our side always had the best pick-pocketing classes.

She had a message from HQ for me, since she was working for us back then. At least I thought she was until I found out what I had to do to get it. That was when I started to wonder. Not that it stopped me. No sir, I applied the finest of American ingenuity at my disposal to the matter at hand. That, and my tongue and fingers, not to mention a few purchases from a tiny little shop a few streets away. Gia came twice in my bed before I got the message out of her, then a few times after that just for the fun of it.

That was the best part so of course it went downhill from there. The orders were for me to go to Caracas and meet a man about some research notes, nothing unusual or interesting. Except that Gia stole the contact information back from me when she snuck out sometime later on that night and the guy in Caracas never showed up. I never figured out exactly why but I could guess.

After that I heard that she'd gone over to the other side. One of the other sides, anyway. I retired a few years later and tried to settle down. But I was restless and still found myself doing a courier job or two from time to time. As I said, old habits die hard. That was what brought me back to Italy, making it easier for old friends and foes to track me down.

A woman wearing dark glasses and a trench coat walked slowly down the street toward the cafe. Gia? The hair was right: jet black with a touch of silver around the temples, a bit grayer that I remembered. This woman's body was rounder than Gia's had been but the swing of the hips certainly brought back memories. I wondered about the sunglasses though, since it was getting dark. But then she was always one to do the unexpected. I smiled in anticipation and uncoiled from my shelter.

As I got closer, the woman lowered her glasses on her nose a smidge and gave me the once over. Not Gia: the nose and chin were all wrong. But perhaps the evening wouldn't be wasted if she didn't show after all. Or did show up and tried to kill me, which would mean I'd be looking for other company. Never hurt to try and plan for all the contingencies.

The other woman's dark-eyed gaze swept from my face down to my toes. I wondered if she liked what she saw, since I couldn't tell from what I could see of her face. "You haven't changed a bit, Nash." The voice that purred out of her lips was pure Gia: lilting Italian accent and all.

I did a very quick double take. "That's some disguise. I didn't recognize you."

She laughed, but not like she thought I'd made a joke. "No disguise, I'm afraid. They had to reconstruct what was left of my face after my car got bombed in Kandahar." She took off the glasses and balanced them on her head. "So...have I lost all my appeal?"

What could I say? This new Gia had a longer face and a less aquiline nose. Her lips were thinner and now that I could see all of her face, I could see the shadow of burn scars on her forehead and neck. But who was I to complain? I had plenty of scars of my own so I said what needed to be said, "Sweetheart, you're gorgeous and you could never be anything but. Now let me buy you dinner and we can get caught up on old times." I tilted my head at the café and gave her my best lady killer grin.

A slow answering smile crossed her face and for a moment, she was the Gia I remembered. She led me over to a distant corner table and we sat down to read the menus by the light of the candle in the Chianti bottle. I noticed she replaced the sunglasses with reading glasses and it made me smile a little. I waved to the waiter. "You still drinking Slings?"

"Perhaps just for tonight," she nodded at the waiter's glance and smiled herself when I ordered my martini. "Still the same old Nash. I'd have thought being a creature of habit would have gotten you killed by now. I'm glad to see that it hasn't."

"Me too. Though somehow I don't remember my habits being as dangerous as yours. I've never betrayed a partner, for example." I leaned against the table, my hand clenching under it to release the tiny gun in my jacket sleeve.

She must've heard the quiet pop of the springs. "Put the silly gun away, Nash. Those days are done. Besides, you didn't think I'd have searched your room without removing most of your bullets, did you?" She extended one long-fingered hand and showed me an assortment of bullets of various calibers and several clips that I recognized as mine.

I glared at her, wondering if it was worth my while to check the chambers on a few of the pieces I was carrying. I decided against it and wondered when she'd found time to search my room. It didn't surprise me much, somehow. "You find anything else of interest?" I asked at last. No point in looking too vulnerable.

"You still carry a picture of me in your wallet." She smiled and it was breathtaking. The shock ran from my eyeballs down below my waist all of a sudden, like a shot of good whiskey. Then I was damp between the legs and I wanted Gia Morelli like I hadn't wanted another woman in years. She pulled in closer to the table and I heard a slight scrape of her high heels on the cobblestones.

I braced myself for knives, razors, whatever it was she had tucked up in her shoes. Instead, one of her bare feet slid its way up my calf. Against my better judgment, I pulled her foot up into my lap. I put my sleeve gun away and caressed her foot, feeling my way carefully over her delicate toes and down her instep. I started massaging her silky skin, rubbing until I could see her face relax and her eyelids droop.

That was when the waiter came back. We didn't move, not like the old days when we would have pulled apart and pretended nothing was going on. I ordered for both of us and he sauntered off with a knowing smile. I kept up my attention to her foot until I thought the time was ripe for answering questions. "So where have you been all these year, babe? And how'd I get so lucky as to have my name pop up on the Rolodex now?"

"Do you still use those?" Her eyebrows soared and she pulled a PDA from her pocketbook and waved it at me before dropping it back in. "I had no idea. Anyway, darling, you know I always meant to call you." She flashed me another bewitching smile and the foot resting in my lap suddenly ground into my very wet crotch.

With an effort, I moved it away and placed it on my knee. I could play hard to get if I had to, and something told me that I needed a few more details before I gave in. "Yet you didn't until now and I've been back in Italy a few times since the old days. So what made you so nostalgic this trip?" I sipped my martini and sized her up.

She leaned forward so that I could see the edge of a lacy bra and more than a hint of ample cleavage. I remembered eating tiramisu from between her breasts and only just managed not to choke on my drink. "I want to take you someplace tonight, Nash. Someplace new that I think you will like. That is why I waited to call you. Can you trust me enough to let it be a surprise? You know I'd never let anything happen to you."

This time, I stared at her in complete disbelief. But maybe it was just the ache of the shoulder wound she gave me back in El Salvador when she was pretending to be with the FMLN instead of the CIA. Or was it the other way around? Who could remember now? Then there was the scar from that time in Moscow. A quick inventory brought up a few other nicks and scrapes from other incidents. Finally I replied, "Babe, a girl could be dead three times over from a few of the love bites you've given me over the years."

Gia gave me an unreadable look. "Patricia, if I wanted to kill you, you'd be dead by now. I do not say this to wound you, only to remind you that I have never harmed you more than necessary." Her mouth was set and she looked very serious, very unGialike for a moment.

What could I do but nod? She wasn't wrong, much as I wanted her to be. I'd gotten her once or twice when a mission required it but I'd never come close to doing serious damage. She, on the other hand, had had plenty of chances to kill me. "All right, you've made your point."

The waiter reappeared again. I kicked myself for not suggesting he make himself scarce. Of course, he brought the food this time so I didn't have much of an excuse to drive him off. But once we had our dinner, I made up for lost time and slipped him a few Euro not to interrupt us until I signaled. He rolled his eyes but took himself off to wait on a group of tourists who had just wandered in.

Gia was tucking into dinner with a healthy appetite, but I couldn't help but notice, not really answering my questions. I caressed her foot, letting her move it gently over the inside of my thigh. I thought about taking her here and now, pulling her onto the table and making love to her in the wreckage of our dinner. I imagined her skirt rucked up around her hips, her sweet naked pussy open and wet. I wondered if the tourists would stay to watch or leave in a huff.

"What are you thinking, Nash? You only smile like that when you think wicked thoughts. But then perhaps I too am thinking wicked thoughts." She gave me a smirk of pure femme power and I started to move her foot away from any area that was going to affect my judgment. She responded by leaning across the table and feeding me a bite of her pasta.

Then she switched feet, running her toes up my thigh until she could see my response in my face. My thoughts got a lot more wicked and we smiled at each other over the candle flame. Gia changed the mood by asking me a few insignificant questions, the whereabouts of old acquaintances and such. But I had read the promise in her eyes and as soon as my dinner was done, I began working my hand from her foot down her calf, caressing and massaging as I went. I even pulled her, chair and all, a bit closer so I reach the sensitive skin above her knee.

It wasn't the way I remembered it though. Too much scar tissue for that, I realized once my fingers recognized what they were caressing. I didn't let it show in my face. She would have seen it as pity and Gia Morelli was not a woman to feel sorry for. I wondered if that was why she called me, hoping to go back to the way she was before the explosion that left her like this.

She didn't move her leg or change her smile but she did snap her fingers for the waiter. He swept away the empty plates, after giving me a wary glance, then trotted off to the kitchen for the inevitable tiramisu. She still had her sweet tooth. "Are you seeing anyone, Nash? I suppose I should have asked earlier but I thought you would have mentioned her by now." She still had the ability to catch me off guard too.

"Why wait until now to ask that? I'd have thought that question was more relevant back before you got me all hot and bothered with your footwork. No, Gia, I'm not currently seeing anyone. How about you? Got a whole houseful of bambinos waiting for you after you have your way with me?"

Her face changed this time, getting older and sadder while I gave myself several swift mental kicks. Finally she looked away and murmured, "No. No bambinos, Nash." She put her foot down and back into her shoe, leaving an ache in my thighs that ran through me like a knife.

If I could have given her a baby then and there, I would have. "Gia, I'm sorry. I didn't mean to hurt you." She raised a hand to stop me and shrugged, the gesture pure Italian. I got nervous, making small talk until dessert showed up; no point in wrecking a perfectly good reunion. She seemed to relax again as we tucked into that marvel of espresso and cream as it can only be made in the land that created it.

Once we finished and I picked up the tab, she let me put her wrap back around her shoulders. Then she tucked her hand through my arm and pulled me from the café out into the plaza. I kept a weather eye out for surprises but I didn't look very hard. Mostly I told her entertaining stories about missions she hadn't been on and watched her laugh as we walked down the winding stone streets. I loved the way she laughed: head thrown back, slightly crooked teeth gleaming in the occasional street lamp. Except they weren't crooked anymore. I was going to miss that about her smile, I realized with a pang.

That was when we got to the place that she was leading me to. Not that the outside of yet another old stone building with an unmarked door told me a thing. Part of my brain registered the address and filed it away for future reference, but there wasn't anything else to notice about it. Except that there were lights on upstairs, which didn't worry me much. There was also a little bit of music in the air, a sound that could have been coming from the house or from the plaza behind us, or just from the sheet joy of looking into Gia's eyes.

She grinned at me and pulled me up the steps to the door. The eyes in the lioness doorknocker met mine and I jumped a little. Gia spoke to it in Italian like it was an old friend and the eyes switched back to being brass, just like that. I had hoped for a quiet evening, just the two of us but it looked like it was going to be a bit more complicated than that. I resigned myself to whatever hopefully nonlethal surprise my charming friend had waiting for me inside.

The door opened slowly, sending a wash of pale golden light out over the steps. I couldn't see the face of whoever was playing butler and Gia was hanging onto the sleeve with the gun in it. If something was wrong, I was in trouble. She pulled me inside with a giggle.

I swore a little under my breath when I saw the woman at the door. For one thing, she was huge. She was also ugly as sin, with an old knife scar running the length of her cheek and a couple of missing teeth. From her expression, she didn't think much of the way I looked either. Gia burbled at her and I caught a few phrases that suggested she was vouching for me. Finally, the giantess nodded and held out her hand for something. "She wants your guns, Nash," Gia said helpfully.

Over my dead body. Which given our relative sizes, it might be. Gia pulled out a dainty little gun, then another. Then pulled up her skirt to turn in a throwing knife and a few other things she kept in her garter. The door guard ran a detector of some kind over her then nodded as she came up clean.

Then it was my turn. Reluctantly, I turned in the sleeve gun. The detector beeped in my general direction. I gave up a few more things. It beeped again and Gia rolled her eyes. One pointed high heel tapped my shin and I grinned like I'd forgotten the gun in the ankle holster.

The detector stopped beeping and I got a begrudging nod. Feeling naked, I trailed after Gia into the hallway. She headed for the stairs, not giving me a lot of time to look around. Not that there was much to see: a few generic landscapes on the walls, a plush, velvety chair or two, a staircase and a couple of closed doors. My eyes narrowed as I studied them until she stopped on her way up. "Bathroom," she said pointing to the left, "Kitchen and library. Open them up if you have to, Nash." Her tone suggested I'd be doing a lot of atoning if I didn't take her word for it.

I shrugged and headed up the stairs behind her. Sometimes old habits are meant to be broken. Besides, nobody lives forever. At least I'd go out wined and dined. Gia shrieked something in Italian as she got to the head of the stairs. I reached for my empty pocket before I realized that it was a happy sound. There was a chorus of laughter and greetings in response that made me raise my eyebrows.

I followed her up, wondering what I'd find up there. Two seconds later I found out. A lithe, gray-haired woman rocketed out of nowhere and seized my hand. "Nash, my favorite American, it is good to see you. We feared you were dead, though Gia always said otherwise." I shook her hand in a daze. Tatiana Tchrenkov. My old foe from the KGB. At least until she became my ally from assorted other agencies.

I glanced over her shoulder and was amazed to see a bunch of familiar faces: Nola Ktana, Li Chen, Maris Cherbourg and a few more whose names I couldn't remember. Every woman agent I could remember from twenty years ago was there, at least all the ones who were still alive. The room was a lot more interesting than the one downstairs too: there was a huge bar for one thing, and a familiar face grinning at me from the other side of it. I grinned back at my old buddy Janice and headed over her way. Gia caught up with me when I got to the bar and gave Janice a steely smile. "You and Nash can catch up later, no? I want to show her the rest of the club."

Janice rolled her dark eyes at me as Gia's head turned and I got towed away before I could do more than mumble at her. I'd forgotten how jealous Gia was of my ex. Not like it wasn't all over years ago. Still, I couldn't help but notice that the years had been kind to Jan. I'd be here a few more days. Maybe we could catch up later. Or so I thought until Gia got me into the next room.

Or next rooms, really. There was a blur of computer rooms, wallscreens and assorted bookshelves, some of which had actual books on them. What can I say? I'm old-fashioned. Judging from the speed we were moving at, none of this was what I was brought here to see. In typical Gia-like fashion, she saved the best for last.

We bolted up the stairs to the third floor before Gia stopped in front of a closed door. She gave me a mysterious smile, then ran one red fingernail down my jaw. Then she pulled my face down to hers and gave me a kiss that warmed every nerve ending in my body. My arms felt like she'd never left them, like they'd been empty for years and were finally full. At that moment, I wanted Gia Morelli more than I'd ever wanted anything or anyone. Except of course, Gia, the last time I'd held her like this.

Then she reached back and opened the door. Whatever I'd been expecting to find on the other side, what I was looking at wasn't it. Mostly I'd been hoping for a nice big bed. What I got instead was a pretty smiling woman wearing some sort of sarong and gesturing us inside. Gia pulled me in while I fumbled for my billfold, certain I could get rid of unwanted company if I had enough cash on me.

I stopped when I saw the rest of the room: two or three massage tables and what looked like the door to a sauna, standard health spa issue. "You've gone to a lot of trouble to get me here if all you want's a massage, babe," I growled the words, disappointment in every syllable.

"Silly Nash. We have many more services than this - it's our club, after all. Anything our members desire, we provide." She snuggled up to me and fluttered her eyelashes. "And I think I know what you want." Her little hands were deftly unbuttoning my shirt while she pulled me along to a door in the far wall.

This time the door swung open on an empty room. Empty, that is, except for the nice big bed in the middle of the room. It even had a canopy and curtains. We stepped inside, but something didn't feel right and I shoved Gia behind me as she closed the door. A blur of motion from the curtains caught my eye. "Down! Take cover!" I yelled as I jumped forward and grabbed the nightstand by the door.

Whatever it was, it picked up speed as I moved and paused when I froze. I dropped to one knee, part of my brain registering that Gia had ducked behind a chair in the corner. Now I could see whatever it was that was tracking us, but the knowledge didn't make me any happier. The tiniest missile I've even seen hovered a few feet away. I wondered if it was set for heat or motion. I sincerely hoped it was motion.

Then I wondered who'd left it for me. Us. Any of the women downstairs might have a reason for it: old grudges, new missions, you name it. Or maybe just orders from on high, nothing personal. Not that that would make us any less dead. I shifted a bit and the missile pointed right at me. Gia threw a pillow into the far corner and it homed in on that. It was smart enough to know that the pillow wasn't its target though so we didn't have much time.

I glanced around without moving my head. The bathroom was off to my right, much closer than the window. I liked my odds of drowning it better than my other option of turning it out into the Italian night. Gia's lips pursed in an air kiss and she gestured slightly. She had figured out what I had in mind and was ready to play along. Or at least that's what I hoped she meant.

The missile was starting to look around. Gia threw another pillow as I dropped and rolled for the bathroom door. I hoped that was enough to confuse it as I uncurled and sprawled my way into the biggest bathroom I'd ever seen. The center was filled with an opulent bathtub with some kind of whirlpool in the middle. It was my lucky night. I hit the tub's switch and froze as the missile darted in the open door behind me.

It wove and spun around the room, seeking for some sign of me. Fortunately, that was the whirlpool jets kicked in. The missile hovered for a second, then dove for the water. I hit the tiles and covered my head as a geyser gushed up out of the tub. In a second, I was soaked to the skin but I stayed put for a minute or two more, just because.

Gia's tap on my elbow made me uncurl. "It's done, Nash. That was marvelous, you haven't lost your touch." She slid forward a little so she was lying on my stomach and chest and kissed me again. The tiles sloshed under me as I got my arms around her and kissed her back. She managed to finish unbuttoning my shirt as I rolled over and got her underneath me. I yanked off my wet jacket and shirt and threw them into a corner, then sent the sports bra there a minute later.

Gia murmured an appreciative noise as she kissed my shoulder. I must be holding up better than I thought. I reached up and started unbuttoning her blouse, but slower and more carefully than she'd done mine. I wanted this to last for awhile, just in case I didn't see her again for a few years. I followed my fingers with my tongue and mouth while she moaned and rocked under me until I ran out of buttons.

Then I pulled her up so she was sitting facing me and reached up to unhook the lacy bra that held her breasts in. She was breathing fast and her eyes met mine with an electric shock that burned right through me. Then she glanced over my shoulder and the biggest smile I'd ever seen lit her face. "Oh! Look at the tub, Nash!"

I turned, a bit warily, I admit. The tub was still whirling away behind us but now the surface was covered with rose petals. A tiny scrap of paper floated on top of the water. I reached over and picked it up and read "Welcome back, old friends," no signature. "Who do you think did this?"

Gia was tugging at the snaps of my pants, her thigh rubbing my crotch through the seam of my pants. I decided to worry about it later and slid my hand up along her thigh under her skirt. She gasped a little and I pulled the skirt higher. She reached back and unfastened it and together we wriggled it up over her head and off. It joined the pile of clothes in the corner along with my pants and the rest of our underwear.

Then I picked her up, slowly and awkwardly and carried her to the side of the tub. We went in together when I slipped, dropping into a wave of hot water and rose petals. Gia giggled as I stroked her beautiful scarred legs on my way into her pussy. She wrapped her legs around my hips and pulled us both down so we were in front of one of the jets. She had one of my nipples in her mouth by then and I was letting the water pressure drive my fingers up inside her, grinning like a fool the whole time.

I twisted a little and she stretched a bit wider so I could get all my fingers inside her wetness. For good measure, I brought up my other hand and slipped a finger into her ass. Somehow I grinned even more when I heard her moan. She always had the best moans; it was like they started in her toes and worked their way up through a couple of miles of Gia before they escaped her lips. I shoved my hands inside her, rocking as much as my old fingers thought they could take, loving how wet she was right now, how much she wanted me.

She arched her back then and came hard, legs shaking around me. For that moment, it was like we were in our thirties again and I wished like anything that it had stayed like this. But then there was something to be said for age and experience. I gave my fingers a wiggle and leaned over to take her nipple in my mouth. She twisted a little so that the water would catch me where it would do the most good.

The jets hit me just right and I came with her, my own orgasm slower and quieter than hers. But she knew and gave me the most gorgeous smile I'd ever seen on her face. She wrapped her scarred legs around me a little tighter and pulled me in close. "I love you, Nash. I always have," she whispered against my ear, then stopped my mouth with a kiss before I could answer.

Part of me wondered what other surprises were floating around the room, besides little missiles filled with rose petals. I wondered what it would be like to trust a lover, any lover, let alone one who'd nearly killed me a half dozen times.

The rest of me wondered if she could make me come a second time, something I almost never managed. Gia's hand found my clit, deft fingers coaxing me to come again while she ran her mouth down my neck. I ran my hands over the faint scars on her back, letting the rough edges turn me on even more. I like a woman who's been around. Her tongue found the old bullet wound in my shoulder and somehow she managed to make it a new erogenous zone. I came, hard, unable to resist giving Gia anything she wanted.

Then I put her up on the edge of the tub and ate her out. I buried my face in her pussy and licked like I could lick away every wound, every betrayal. I lost track of how many times she bucked and writhed, her legs stiffening and shaking around me. She was calling my name amid strings of Italian, endearments as well as the occasional curse when it finally got to be too much and she pushed me away so she could slide back into the water.

She stroked my cheek and I could tell that she was waiting for a response. Did I love her? I wanted to think so but I wasn't sure. This time, instead of saying what needed to be said, I looked at Gia and murmured the first thing that popped into my head, "Kid, this could be the beginning of a beautiful friendship." She threw her head back and laughed while I kissed her neck. At least I was sure that I loved to watch her laugh.

Medusa's Touch

TiCara walked down the corridor as if she owned the place, not like the secur cams and even the Eyes were watching her every move. She never looked back at them, not even when one of the Eyes scuttled out almost under her foot. Let the other corps wonder why she was here. The speculation would be good for business. If they assumed that she was in demand, they'd try to hire her for their own jobs. She hoped.

When she reached the end of the hall, Sherin Chan was waiting for her, just like TiCara knew she would be. Not that the rep was ever anything other than coolly professional but TiCara hadn't worked the spacer bars when she was a kid for nothing. She knew desire when she saw it.

She met Sherin's dark eyes and stopped way too close for comfort, her face centimeters from the other woman's. "Hello, Sherin," she breathed. "Good to see you." She ran a finger down the rep's blacksuit as if she was going to unfasten it and Sherin stepped back looking alarmed.

TiCara gave her a predatory grin and gestured toward the doorway. "Trin Vahn wants me now. You can have me later." Sherin looked away, her breathing just the tiniest bit faster and TiCara's grin widened a bit before she pulled her mouth into the sobriety appropriate for a meeting like this one. Sherin hit the door's secur button with a grimace and ushered her in, careful not to meet her eyes a second time.

Trin Vahn sat behind his desk looking even more ancient than he had a few months ago at their last meeting. Word from the Eyes was that Eternayouth didn't affect him, that he would die a wizened old man while his rivals outlived him. Or so they all hoped. Personally, TiCara was hoping for him to outlast them all, mostly because his credit was always good.

She made the formal United Systems greeting: hand to heart to lips to forehead, followed by a bow. It was more formal than she really needed with an established client but it would help sweeten up the old man. She looked up and he nodded in acknowledgement before he spoke, "I have need of your services, TiCara. I apologize for the short notice but this is important."

It must be. Vahn had never gone straight to business in all the years that she'd dealt with him. He also made no mention of Sirius Transport, the shipping corps she currently contracted for, only her. She smoothed her surprise away with a smile and a sweeping gesture. "Of course, Ser. Any services I can provide are yours." *For a price, of course.* She dropped her eyes demurely, then shot a sideways glance at Sherin. The other woman watched her employer as if he was the only thing in the room, dark eyes fixed so firmly on him they might have been glued in place.

Vahn spoke again, his voice that of a weary old man. "You have heard the stories they tell in the spacer bars about Electra 12, have you not?"

TiCara's eyebrows rose, or might have if she still had any. The effect was nearly the same. "I have heard the stories, of course. But they say the asteroid's a myth, Ser." Electra 12 was supposed to be an artificial asteroid where the hot springs rejuvenated old bodies back to their youth, where you could find a cure for almost any illness and a dozen more tales besides, each wilder than the last. Gossip said that the location was secret but could be obtained for a big enough price. She looked at Vahn sympathetically; only a dying man would pursue a dream as futile as this one.

"It is not a myth. I have spoken to reliable sources who tell me that some of the benefits of the asteroid are true, as are the stories about its hidden location," Vahn leaned forward in his chair, eyes piercing now. "I need you to get me there."

This time, TiCara didn't bother to hide her astonishment. Vahn had his own ships, any one of them bigger and faster than her *Ad Astra*. She generally used her ship for smuggling and black-market work, sometimes even hauling legitimate freight, but never passengers. Especially not rich ones.

She surprised herself by speaking her thoughts aloud. "My ship is always available to you, Ser but why not take one of your own?" A moment later it struck her. Vahn didn't want anyone in his corps to know what he was up to. If they knew he was vulnerable, he could lose his position, his cred, even his life. In some parts of the galaxy, the Corporate Wars had never ended. Which meant that this might be a one way trip for her and her crew.

Something of her fear must have shown on her face, despite the years she had spent disciplining herself to show only what she wanted others to know. Vahn sounded amused when he answered, "TiCara, don't you know me better than that? I will pay well for your search, better for your silence. There is nothing to be afraid of. Please go and prepare your ship. I ask that you tell the crew nothing for now. I don't want the Eyes to know anything until we arrive on Electra and my treatments have begun."

He paused and gave TiCara an unreadable glance before he continued, "I want to leave within two cycles. Sherin will handle the navigation coordinates and my needs, you will attend to all the other logistics and serve as pilot. My credit is open to you: take what you need. Consider your silence already paid for." He leaned back, his eyes closing in a seemingly involuntary gesture.

TiCara didn't really believe that he felt that old, that sick. It was meant only to sooth her terrors and she felt ashamed that she needed to see it. But his credit was good and Sherin Chan looked almost as good as the credit. The other woman glanced up, catching her eye, her desire clear and naked for an instant. TiCara smiled, letting her anticipation show. Her last few jobs had come at a high price: lost creds, lost crew, lost loves. Perhaps this one would be what she needed to forget all that.

She made the appropriate responses to Vahn, doing all that the old man would have wanted in the way of a formal parting. Then she followed Sherin from the room, watching the other woman's body in her form-fitting suit. This might be even good enough for old-fashioned meat space sex, something better than just jacking into the VR modules. She imagined the taste of Sherin's skin, the feel of flesh against flesh, and it intrigued her, sending warm ripples though her body.

The door closed behind them and Sherin stopped, turned to say something through blackberry lips gone puffy and delectable. TiCara stepped up to her and, after a moment's hesitation, kissed her. She could feel Sherin tremble, feel the first tentative fumblings of the rep's tongue against hers. It struck her then that this beautiful woman had never known sex outside of the VR mods and the realization jolted her. This job could be so much more than she had hoped for when she entered Vahn's office. She could feel herself get slick with the thought and deepened the kiss, parting Sherin's teeth with her tongue and pulling her close.

But she had preparations to make and profit was never far from her mind. After a moment or two, she pulled back from the kiss, sending out a single medusa wire from the headset wired into her skull to stroke the other woman's cheek. Sherin shuddered and half-closed her eyes, as if TiCara had touched her herself instead of using the wired in mobile hookups from her equipment. "We've got work to do, my shiny pretty. Fun must wait, sadly." Reluctantly she stepped backward, the medusa lingering for an instant longer than necessary.

Sherin's eyes were half-closed and TiCara could see the breath catch in her throat. Then the corps rep training took over and a layer of ice spread over her features. "Of course. Follow me please." Sherin turned on her heel and walked down the hall, only a quick, savage kick at an Eye that came too close conveying her frustration.

She missed but the gesture made TiCara smile just a little, though her disappointment was visible in the line of her mouth. She hating postponing her pleasures, especially the more unusual ones. But business needed to come first. She followed the other woman to her office where Sherin handed her a credchip. "Try not to blackhole his cred." She almost smiled then seemed to think the better of it and looked stern. "I run the numbers for him. I'll know if you exceed what's needed."

"As if I would break one of my best clients. Silly shiny girl. Give me a kiss before I head?" TiCara stepped up to the rep's side but hesitated at her glare and settled for running a finger down her cheek. She reveled in the blush that followed, darkening Sherin's skin from deep gold to dark brown in an instant. Then she backed away, chip in hand, her smile promising more to come later.

But for now, she needed no distractions. First, she needed to know more about Electra. Then she needed to round up the crew, buy fuel and take care of the thousand other preparations this kind of journey would involve. The purchase of personal weapons, for example. Not that she didn't want to trust Vahn but she hadn't lasted this long as a pilot-captain of her own ship without learning to prepare.

She found a com and used the medusas from her headset to send a message to her second, Erol. The medusas would mix her brainwaves with their own signal to make it harder for anyone to hack the call, just in case someone was paying attention. Erol promised that he would get started on supplies and fuel, just as she expected. Now she needed information and there was only one source that she trusted to give her what she needed.

She headed for Downside, the spacer colony under Kyrin's surface. Vishistory said Downside was Downside because Upside cost too many creds but TiCara knew how badly spacers needed to get away from the endless sky for awhile. She'd spent plenty of time jacked into the pilot's chair, staring out into the never-never of the starfields. Underground had limits, boundaries, and she craved it as much as any of the other spacers.

The dark closed in around her as the gravitube dropped down to the next level. It was really only dark in comparison to Upside but that was enough. The walls around her sparkled a little from the tubelights, the residue of some mineral left over from Kyrin's past as a mining colony as were the shafts themselves. She grinned a little to herself as the tube stopped and she stepped out onto the walkway that ran the length of the shaft that led to the bars and hostels. This was home, almost as much as the *Astra*.

The walkways were crowded this time in the cycle but then Kyrin was a big enough port that they were never deserted. She walked along purposefully, careful to glance sidelong at passersby without making eye contact. The meeting of eyes was an invitation to sex, violence, a dozen other things. She knew better now than to be drawn to that kind of fun.

Ahead of her, she noticed a pair of Ears with a pack of Eyes at their heels looking her way. One of them trailed after her when she passed them. Word of today's meeting must have spread. She didn't let her anger show but it was still hard not to shake the corps agent off.

She reminded herself that all he would learn by following her was that she liked to drink in spacer bars and had a few friends there, nothing more. She let the thought of his frustration ease her annoyance as she slipped into The Haven and looked around for Elia. The old pilot was always here when she was awake and TiCara knew that if anyone knew much about Electra, it would be Elia.

She also knew Elia's price, the knowledge making her breathe a tiny bit faster. It wouldn't be like being with Sherin, or what she hoped being with Sherin would be like, but it would be excellent preparation. One of the medusas from her headset caught her mood and caressed her neck, its little glowing eye programmed to know which areas would get the most reaction from her or her lovers.

Elia was there, just as she anticipated. But she wasn't alone. There was an Ear sitting with her and he looked familiar. It was the one who had disappeared from the dock, leaving his friend to tail her. His lips curled into an almost smile when he saw TiCara and she grimaced in return. The medusa drew back as her mood shifted from aroused to wary. She pursed her lips at Elia in an all purpose greeting and promise. Elia smiled back and nodded to the Ear. "'Lo TiCara. Know Zig?"

Zig touched a hand to his forehead by way of greeting. Then he glanced back at Elia. "Info is cred, pilot. You know what I need." He slid out of his chair and walked away without looking at either of them again.

TiCara looked directly into Elia's eyes as she sat down. "What was that? You work for the corps now?" Her lip curled a little when she said it, almost as if she might smile. But she didn't. Elia never dealt much with the corps before; if she was doing it now, maybe it would be better not to ask about Electra. TiCara always tried to steer clear of corps politics.

Elia smiled and stood up, her body straight and elegant despite her years, and leaned across the table to kiss her. The movement startled TiCara and her lips parted under Elia's, more surprised than desirous for the moment. A medusa from Elia's headset reached out and twined itself in among hers and a shudder ran through her. Elia didn't answer her question, choosing instead to break off the kiss before catching her arm and towing her toward the stairs at the back of The Haven's main room. Privacy for this talk then, TiCara decided and didn't ask again.

Besides, it wasn't as though she didn't have other things on her mind right now. The kiss had melted her in a way that she hadn't expected, as if the touch of Elia's tongue had turned her body into something that floated like a creature from one of the lowgrav worlds. Every medusa on her head strained after Elia until TiCara forced them back into the semblance of hair. Elia glanced back and smiled at her as they went up the stairs, her expression making it clear that this was more than just a quick exchange of sex for information.

She followed Elia into one of the VR rooms at the top of the stairs and watched as she sealed the securlock behind them. For a moment, it made her think of Sherin and how different this moment would have been with her. But being with Elia was part of coming home too; they had done this dance many times before, so often now that she thought of it as part of being home in Downside.

Elia was already plugging herself into the VR modules and TiCara found herself doing the same. The VR's medusa sockets embraced their followed her lead on their own pallet. She could feel herself get wet in her blacksuit, could feel the line of heat running from her sex down her thighs and up into her belly. For a moment, she just lay there, enjoying the sensation of unfulfilled wanting,

Then she reached for Elia's avatar, wrapping her legs around the older woman's as she tilted her face up for a kiss. Elia's tongue was gentle in her virtual mouth, exploring it as if it was somehow new this time. She cupped her hand over Elia's full breast and squeezed, coaxing her nipple into rock hardness. The other pilot gasped from her bed and TiCara twisted around to bite her nipple through the blacksuit.

A moment later, TiCara felt Elia's hand between her legs. She pulled Elia close as the medusas fed the other pilot's image and the sensation of her touch, her scent, directly into her brain. This was the beauty of the VR mods, at least as far as TiCara was concerned. It was so direct, so safe, with none of the risks of meatspace sex.

Then there were the other benefits. There was something between Elia's legs now, some kind of appendage that hardened like a real penis. The feeling made TiCara wetter than she'd thought possible and Elia rubbed herself against TiCara's hip, riding the sensation that swept from TiCara's mind into her own and back.

The feedback loop dragged a moan out of TiCara and all of her clothing dropped away from her avatar like an old skin. Elia's hands were hard on TiCara's hips, yanking her on top so that she could feel Elia's breasts against her own. She reached down between Elia's legs past the avatar's thickening member and buried her fingers in Elia's wet pussy. Elia groaned, reaching out to slip her own fingers inside TiCara's aching wetness. TiCara's hips rocked forward in response, riding her hand for a few moments.

Then Elia pulled her fingers out of TiCara and shifted her body around until she could work her penis inside her. TiCara moaned and gasped for air at the unexpected sensation. Elia didn't feel completely artificial or completely real inside her but was somehow a little of both. She shoved TiCara up and back so that she was sitting on her erection. TiCara wailed and reached for her own breasts as Elia's fingers found her clit.

The sensations were almost enough to overcome TiCara's surprise. Elia was a competent lover but she had never done something like this before. Reveling in the unusual, she rode Elia rocking her hips until the pressure of Elia's fingers and the stroking of her penis inside her made her collapse shaking on the other woman's body. Elia grabbed her hips and rocked inside her a few more times until she bucked under TiCara's body, coming with a final thrust.

TiCara could feel Elia's member deflate slowly inside her and the sensation sent a final shiver through her. Elia must have felt it through the medusas and she rolled them over, sliding down until she was between TiCara's legs. She ran her tongue slowly over TiCara's clit, then pulled the little nub of flesh between her teeth and sucked hard. TiCara felt a whitehot flash shoot through her and her entire body shook, bucking frantically against Elia's mouth until she could feel the other woman laughing through the medusa link.

TiCara yanked her medusas from the VR plugs and sat up on her pallet. She was disoriented and her body still shook a little but now she suspected that Elia was using sex to avoid her questions. The thought angered her more than it should have since they had no connection that the other pilot need honor beyond friendship. She glared at Elia as the other woman sat up and gently unplugged her own medusas.

Elisa gave her a gently amused smile. "Thought you'd like that. So what did you come to query me about, Ti?" She sat Buddha-style on the pallet, medusas coiling themselves around each other as if their owner had no concerns beyond a social talk.

TiCara growled under her breath before she answered. Time to rein in all she felt. Elia would think she was upset about Zig. Let it seem like jealousy or uncertainty about the Ears, nothing more than that. "One, tell me what you were doing with the Ear, El. Got no more words until then." She found herself sliding into spacer talk, with its clipped words and short sentences once she got Downside. It was different from the way she talked to clients but here it felt like a second skin.

Elia kept smiling. "Ears got no home once they work for the corps, Ti? I know Zig 'fore you got wired." TiCara stiffened and Elia stopped smiling before she spoke again. "Zig needed Eartalk, needed to know which corps were making queries." Her lips clamped shut as if to hold back anything more.

TiCara tilted her head to one side and asked anyway, "What queries, El? Was info I need know?" The other pilot shook her head but didn't say anything else. The silence stretched between them for long seconds until TiCara touched her hand to her heart to indicate that she trusted the other pilot. Elia did the same and they smiled at each other for a moment.

"What else you need, Ti?" Elia asked, her eyes curious.

"Electra 12. Know it?" Elia looked startled, but only for an instant before something settled into the shadow of her eyes. TiCara filed that away for later thought. She listened as the other pilot told her what she knew, not much more than what Vahn had told her really. A few more details here and there, some of which might be useful, might be just story telling.

There was one thing that stood out though. TiCara's eyes narrowed in the middle of one story about a pilot who'd found Electra and was somehow healed of his/her/zir medusas by the asteroid. The idea made her sick. The brainwired headsets were what made a pilot a pilot. Damage to the medusas could kill you: wiring was for life. Besides, how could you stand to live without them? "How could ze lose zir medusas and not die? Sounds like a VR story, Elia."

Elia shrugged. "Once wired, always wired, far as I know, Ti. But it's what's said."

They talked a bit more after that, but not about Electra 12. When they left the VR room, TiCara even kissed Elia though it wasn't something they did often in meat space. But it felt like the right way to say a temporary farewell. At least that's what TiCara hoped she was doing. Elia held her close a moment longer than she expected and whispered something that TiCara didn't quite hear. Then she stepped back and walked away without saying anything more.

TiCara watched her go and wondered what she had to be afraid of. The Ears, always. If they wanted Vahn dead, they could sabotage her ship or have her killed anywhere, Downside or Upside. The corps had their own laws and they weren't written for pilots on the dark side of legit trade. But she couldn't have attracted that much notice, could she? Except that one of them had been talking to her lover while another one followed her down the walkways.

Her instincts made her wary and she went to one of the other bars before she called Erol. He'd not only gotten supplies, he'd found her two other crewmembers. They were all waiting for her at the *Astra*. She smiled a little and messaged Sherin. The rep's beautiful face danced before her as she told her that everything was almost ready. The rep sent nothing more than agreement back before signing off.

TiCara smiled a little before slipping off into a spacer market in a side cave. She stopped at one of the stands and said a word to the woman who ran it. Credit exchanged hands and she got a small lazergun from a rack under the table. The seller even threw in a few old Earth-style knives and TiCara left feeling a little better. But for the first time since she got her pilot's chip and her medusas, she pulled up her hood to cover them before walking through Downside. The Ears would be looking for a pilot if they were looking for anyone at all. No point in making it easy for them.

She took the long way around to the port on Upside, sending a short message to Erol that she was on her way. No one seemed to be following her but she still breathed a sigh of relief once she reached the *Astra*. Erol was waiting for her, along with Chong and Vijay. She told them only what she had to, then let them get back to work.

She spent the next cycle watching the shadows while she got the ship prepped. Not that there was anything to see, other than a brief glimpse of Zig. But he didn't come near the ship and he didn't seem interested in her so she told herself to stop worrying. It wasn't enough.

Still when Sherin, Vahn and Vahn's bodyguards finally came on board, she was ready for them. The *Astra* had a few extra pulse cannons and considerably more cushions than it had had on its last trip. She hoped they would both be all they needed.

Once the old man was settled into his quarters, she went to find Sherin to get the coordinates. The rep was talking to Erol on the bridge when TiCara got there and the pilot stopped to watch her for a moment. She was relaxed, smiling, at least until she realized she was being watched. Then she turned corps rep cold in an instant.

It made TiCara laugh a little inside; the rep must want her very badly to be exerting this much control. She felt a warm haze of anticipation at the thought. But they needed to get into space first and out past the asteroid belt before she could put the ship on autopilot and do anything about it. "Coordinates?" She made her tone disinterested, not letting it or her face telegraph what she was feeling.

Sherin hesitated a moment before producing a chip from an inner pocket and handing it over. "I'll want that back." She didn't meet TiCara's eyes but she went on standing next to the pilot's chair like she was waiting for something.

All the groundies want to see how the medusas work TiCara thought, stopping her hand before she made a dismissive gesture. *Well, let's see how she likes it.* She stretched out in the pilot's chair and felt the hood begin to settle down. The visor was clear so Sherin could watch as the medusa cables rose gently and fit themselves into the hood's sockets. From there, TiCara could meld with the ship, maneuvering as close to the speed of thought as the technology could get. Medusa ships were small and fast, built for war and fast transport and certain kinds of trade and the *Astra* was one of the best.

With the part of her brain not starting up the ship's functions and getting clearance to go, she noticed that Sherin was looking at her in what seemed like horrified fascination. "This isn't all they're good for," she leered at the other woman but stopped before adding anything more. Let the rest of it be a surprise. She smiled to herself as Sherin turned on her heel and walked away.

After that, it was all about getting the ship out of port and on its way. Chong would see to the passengers and Erol and Vijay would see to everything else. TiCara lost herself in the ship, feeling her way over it like it was part of her own body. She loved this part more than anything else, the power of it as much as the rush that came with it. For the next while, there was no Sherin, just TiCara and her ship.

She flew them out of port, then out past the inner asteroid belt. She used Sherin's chip to enter the coordinates and surprised herself by taking the chip out to return it. Initially she had thought about using it to lure Sherin to her room, but now that seemed silly. She had already hooked the rep so why play games? She was smiling when Erol came to relieve her at the end of her shift.

She stood up and stretched sinuously after her medusas unhooked themselves from the pilot sockets. Erol took the chair. He wasn't wired yet but he could handle the ship on the autopilot and signal her if there was trouble. That sounded just fine to TiCara; she had passengers to attend to. She swept off the bridge, heading first to the quarters she had made up for Vahn to make sure the old man was settling in all right.

After she finished with him, she went looking for his rep. She eventually found Sherin standing by herself in the crew lounge looking out the port glass at the star fields. The rep's expression was wistful, her face tilted back to display her beautiful profile. TiCara hesitated for a moment, breath catching in her throat as she watched her. She wondered what it was that made the other woman look so sad.

The moment didn't last long; Sherin realized she was being watched and turned to meet her eyes. There were tears welling in the rep's eyes but she blinked them away angrily. TiCara stepped forward and reached for her. Sherin flinched away, then slumped into her embrace and let the pilot hold her. She rested her face on TiCara's shoulder and TiCara could feel her sob a little.

TiCara held her for a long moment, holding back her questions. Suddenly Sherin planted a tentative kiss on the exposed skin of her neck, then followed it with a gentle swipe of her tongue. TiCara gasped at the unexpected contact before she twisted her face to the rep's to kiss her. The kiss was less fumbled than the first one, but TiCara could still taste tears in Sherin's mouth.

For a moment, she thought about stopping, getting the rep to share her sorrows. But she suspected that Sherin wouldn't tell her the truth, at least not until she won her trust. Besides she'd had sex to forget before, and sometimes that was all that would be needed or offered. She slid her tongue inside Sherin's mouth and reached up to unfasten the top of the rep's blacksuit.

She could feel Sherin stiffen, then press her body closer as she broke the kiss off. The rep began clumsily unfastening her pilot's jacket, kissing her way over TiCara's exposed skin. TiCara reached up and released Sherin's long black hair from the clasp that held it in place. She buried her hands in its ebony length, using it to pull Sherin's face up and back, arching her neck and shoulders.

Her fingers ran across the rep's skull, the skin rough as if it was scarred from something. The rep went very still as TiCara twisted her medusas down, letting them caress Sherin's neck and jaw with a dozen tiny electric kisses. The rep shuddered in her arms, huge dark eyes closed as if she couldn't bear to watch but wouldn't break away.

TiCara unfastened her blacksuit to the waist, exposing Sherin's full, dark nippled breasts. A lone medusa stroked its way down to one of her nipples, sending the smallest of shocks through the sensitive skin. Sherin wailed then, a sound of loss and desire. TiCara followed the cable with her mouth, drawing her tongue slowly along the same path down Sherin's neck and pulling the rep's hardened nipple into her mouth. She could feel Sherin's heartbeat race under her mouth as she let all of her medusas trace their way over the rep's skin.

Sherin shivered as TiCara dropped one hand down between her legs, caressing her through the blacksuit. The rep moaned then, a sound that shook her from head to toe and TiCara smiled a little. She maneuvered Sherin back to the long low table and stretched her out on it. She didn't resist, dropping backward as if her body had no bones left. Her eyes were still closed and TiCara could see a tear lingering at the edge of one.

She climbed up on the table and kissed it away. Sherin's hands were tugging at her shirt, dragging it off with TiCara's help. Her hands were fierce on TiCara's skin, her touch rough. She kissed TiCara hard and invaded her tongue with her mouth. Her arms were like steel bands holding TiCara in place.

Now it was TiCara's turn to gasp for air as Sherin pulled at the catch to her pants. The rep opened her eyes for a moment, her expression unreadable as she rolled the pilot off her and twisted sideways so that she could pull her pants off. TiCara moaned a little; she had forgotten how good this could be outside the VR mods.

Sherin rolled off the table onto the cushioned bench that ran behind it. She pulled TiCara around so that she could reach her wet slit with her mouth. Then she dropped her face between the pilot's legs and licked as if she had always known how to do this.

TiCara bucked at the touch of her tongue and groaned, "Inside me. Please." She could feel Sherin shift a little, then drive her tongue and a finger up into the aching wetness inside her. TiCara humped her mouth, hips rocking and driving upward. Sherin's thumb found her clit and pressed down hard, barely moving but it was enough that TiCara gave herself up with a shout. She came hard, her hips heaving under Sherin's mouth.

The rep withdrew for a moment, kissing the skin of her thighs while TiCara shivered. Then she drove her hand into the pilot's aching wetness, fastening her mouth to TiCara's clit with the same motion. Her hand was relentless, filling TiCara until the pilot came again with a shout that was nearly a scream. Sherin pulled away then, resting her cheek on TiCara's thigh so that the pilot could feel her breathing, feel her heart race.

TiCara lay still for a moment searching for the air to recover before she tried to pull the rep onto the table with her. Sherin pulled away, shuddering. "You'd use these," she gestured at the medusas, "and I'm not ready yet." She stood up, fastening her blacksuit before she fled, almost running out of the lounge and leaving TiCara staring after her.

The rep avoided her for longer than TiCara would have thought possible on a ship the size of the *Astra*. Eventually, the pilot had to sleep before she went back on shift, then she needed to work. Much as she wanted Sherin, she knew her priorities. There was Vahn to consider as well. The old man did not look well and TiCara had little faith in the coordinates, bought with good cred or not.

But she was distracted enough that it wasn't until her second shift that she noticed something she should have noticed earlier. There was a signal beacon hidden in the dark recess of the cargo bay, tagging their location. She went down by herself and disabled it, not telling any of the crew about it. Erol was nearly wired and she doubted that whoever planted the beacon had his price. The others, crew and passengers alike, she was less sure about. Sherin seemed loyal to Vahn but something certainly had her shaken. Maybe the thought of betraying her employer to the Ears of other corps was what was wrong.

TiCara took the disabled beacon back with her to her temporary quarters and hid it carefully. Even without it, there was a ship in the lanes behind them the next time she checked the view screens. It might be nothing: this was a busy trade point for the system but it was still enough to give her a bad feeling. She told Erol, hoping she'd judged him right and on alternating shifts they watched to make sure the ship wasn't coming within cannon range. It never did, eventually turning off for one of the inner planets.

But on Erol's next shift, there was a new ship, bigger and faster than the previous one, trailing them. That was when TiCara decided that Sherin had hidden out long enough. Vahn wasn't likely to tell her who was following them but the rep might. She plugged her medusas into the spare pilot's helmet in her quarters and sent her senses through the ship, checking for more beacons on the way.

She found Sherin sleeping on a bench in one of the tiny rooms that could be converted for either passengers or cargo. TiCara unplugged herself and headed down two levels. The rep opened her eyes as the door slid open and for the first time, she seemed afraid. The pilot made a face but didn't hesitate as she walked across the room and dropped her body onto the bench so that Sherin was pinned under her. "Hello pretty."

TiCara let her medusas drape themselves down so that they lay along Sherin's neck and jaw. The rep shuddered as they stroked their way slowly over her skin. The look in her eyes told TiCara some of what she needed to know. "Are the Ears behind us, pretty? Did you tell them where we're going with your little beacon?"

Sherin shifted under her, closing her eyes as if to close out the questions. TiCara sent a shock down the medusas, just enough to bite a little. Holding the rep like this was distracting and she could feel herself moisten. She bit Sherin's neck lightly and sent two of the medusas down the collar of her blacksuit, sparking a little as they went.

The rep shuddered under her, shoving her thigh up against TiCara's crotch. "Please," Sherin mumbled, "I'll give you anything you want. Anything at all. Just don't tell Vahn." Her eyes opened now and there was a look of utter desolation in them. But her thigh rocked up into TiCara and the pilot could feel her hands on her hips. She rode the rep's leg for a moment, letting the sensation run through her like a wave.

Then she pulled back. "Tell me why first, pretty. Cred I understand but he's my client now and aboard my ship. Blown all over the never-never's not where I want to be so tell me who and why. Lightspeed now, shiny one. There's not much time. Are the coordinates good?" TiCara nuzzled Sherin's jaw as she spoke, lowering her head so that the medusas could reach all of the rep's throat.

Sherin's breath was coming in gasps. She pressed her lips to TiCara's in an urgent kiss, opening her legs and wrapping them around the pilot's hips. Her hands caressed TiCara's breasts as if she was searching for whatever it took to make TiCara forget her betrayal.

This time, it took a huge effort to pull away enough to meet Sherin's eyes, to stare into them until the rep broke. But this was her ship and the ship behind them could destroy it easily unless she could get them away. Finally Sherin answered, "Yes, but I didn't tell them I knew the coordinates, just planted their beacon. I told them only Vahn knew the coordinates. I had to...I had to do it. You should understand." She caught TiCara's hand and brought it up to her scalp, rubbing her fingers on the scars.

TiCara gave her a look of pure horror. "You're the one, the pilot that the asteroid cured of her medusas. Elia told me about you. That's why you had the coordinates; you'd been there before. Did she bring you to the Ears and they promised you new ones?"

Sherin nodded as she met the pilot's pitying look. TiCara pulled her medusas back so they weren't touching the rep's skin. "No, don't stop. It's too much but it's better than nothing," Sherin whispered. "Elia knew me from before...it happened. She wanted to help, said not to trust the Ears too much but I've got to. They won't do anything until we get there; it's just Vahn they're after."

Right. Because Ears starting a big nova corps war will want lots of witnesses. "Sure they won't, pretty. But no stress to you if I go make things all shiny-sparkly to be positive, right?"

Sherin twisted a little and TiCara found her own lazergun pressed under her chin. "I can't let you do that, Ti. I'm sorry; I don't want to hurt you but this is my last chance. The other rewires all failed, you see. That's why Elia tried to help me. I've got to go into the never-never again. Can't take it planetside much longer." Those big dark eyes had a mad gleam in them now and it sent a shiver through TiCara when she met them. To make it worse, she ran a trembling hand through the pilot's medusas.

The sensation nearly made TiCara's throat close. With an effort she got control of her face and her voice. "Okay, pretty. Whatever you say. Put the gun away and we'll just be together for a little while til we make Electra. Then we'll get you all wired up again." She used the voice that usually worked on mean drunks back in the spacer bars Downside, hoping it might work this time too. Sherin faltered, the gun falling back just a little.

TiCara's medusas reached out and wrapped her fingers around it, freezing them in place so she couldn't fire it easily. Then one slid up and drove its way inside the gun, effectively plugging it. "No," Sherin whispered as the resulting shock tore through her. Her body bucked under TiCara's as the pilot twisted the gun out of her grasp and coiled the medusas back.

TiCara grabbed the gun and rolled off the rep as Sherin curled around herself crying. The pilot ran for the door, racing up the corridor then the ladder to the bridge as fast as she could go. Erol was just pressing the button to com her as she came in. The pursuing ship was coming in range.

Her second jumped out of the chair like he was jet propelled and TiCara dropped into it, pulling the pilot's helm down over the medusas as they plugged themselves in. "Who are they, Ti?" Erol stood awaiting orders, his eyes darting to the *Astra*'s small weapons control panel.

"Ears are onto us. Corps war brewing." TiCara told him. He didn't ask anything more, just stepped over to the panel and start readying their small arsenal. "Tell the load to stay put." She added, knowing he'd know what to do. Then she lost herself in the ship, flying like she'd never flown before. She dodged in front of a big old freighter, ignoring the warning crackle of the com channels. She wove her way in and around a dozen other ships and swung behind an outer moon that orbited one of the gas giants further out in the system.

She used the planet's orbit to kick her around and out beyond the moons into the system's secondary asteroid belt. They spun and wove between the debris until their pursuer fell back. TiCara pulled them into temporary shelter near a big asteroid. An asteroid with what looked like a small port on it in an area where her nav computer said there where no ports. She stared at it in disbelief, then checked their coordinates to confirm it. She made a few more sweeps to make sure their pursuit was gone before she hailed the portship in front of them. "*Ad Astra* carrying passengers to Electra. Permission to dock?"

There was more to it than that of course but after she identified them, dropping Vahn's name and mentioned creds, they were in. She sent her ship into the dock, her body nearly limp with relief. Part of her brain could feel Sherin still huddled in the hold and she spent a moment wondering what she'd do without her medusas. She should tell Vahn what the rep had tried to do; it was her duty as a responsible pilot-owner in his employment.

But she remembered the look in Sherin's eyes and the feel of her body in her arms. She wanted the rep again, wanted to touch her and taste her and feel her shake with ecstasy, maybe even fall in love. She looked at the viewport at the asteroid. Electra 12 could cure almost anything or so Elia had said. Maybe even fixing the craziness it caused.

Vahn was paying well for this trip and the creds should be enough for a treatment or two for his rep. Sherin's gratitude was a given either way. If the asteroid could cure her again, that gratitude might prove very worthwhile. TiCara smiled a grin of pure anticipation as she got up from the pilot's chair and went out looking for Sherin.

THURSDAYS AT MCKINNEY'S

I hadn't always wondered what it would be like to be with another girl. Nossir, I thought I was a straight arrow, got me a boyfriend and everything. And it's not like there were a lot of dykes hanging out at McKinney's. That's the bar where I used to work, waitressing or bartending, depending on the night, to put myself through school. I got nothing against dykes, mind you. I just never gave a lot of thought to them one way or the other.

Not that I had much inspiration, at least not until I got a look at the couple that started coming in every Thursday night. But those two, the brunette and her buddy, something about them was enough to make me reconsider. I mean it wasn't like they were the prettiest girls at the bar or anything so I really don't know what the deal was. But I watched them plenty to try and figure it out, let me tell you. The brunette was big and curvy, with a kind of pretty face and really long brown hair. Her buddy was nothing special to look at. She had sort of shaggy blond hair and glasses, the expensive wire rim kind. She always wore pants and looked like she worked out or something.

I don't know how I figured out they were together that way. I mean they could have been just pals, you know? But there was something in the way they looked at each other, the way that they would touch sometimes, just a little. But enough to make me think about what was going on the rest of the time.

I liked to watch the blonde's hands. They were big hands for a woman, all long fingers with short nails. She had this way of moving them around when she talked, like they were an extra mouth or something, backing up everything she said. After a while I started to wonder what they would feel like inside me. Scared the crap out of me the first time it happened. That was when I knew something was up, and it didn't much matter if it was Johnny or not.

Johnny's the boyfriend I was talking about before, only now he's my fiancé. He's got fantasies of his own, especially that girl on girl stuff. Yeah, he really likes that. Every once in awhile he'll show up at my place with a couple of videos. There's always one of those in the stack. Guess he figures if I watch enough porn, I'd break down and bring one of my girlfriends over and put on a show for him. Fat chance. I mean he always denies it but I know how hot he gets after he watches them. One night I even gave him a lap dance and I am still not sure if it was me or the plastic babes on the tube that got him off.

So when it came to the whole girl-on-girl thing, I guess I just figured that those kind of girls were the only option. You know how it is, they look fake and they act fake so there was nothing about watching them that really grabbed me. Plus, no way was I letting somebody with nails that long put them inside me, even if it was just in my imagination. Gives me the shivers just thinking about it.

These two weren't like that, or at least they didn't look that way to me. The brunette now, she did have kind of long red nails, the kind that came out of a shop where they did them up right, not scary long. They looked nice when she touched the blonde's arm with them. She did that a lot, just resting her hand near the other one's arm, then moving over to grab it or brush against her hand or whatever. Then she'd kind of pull back, play with her hair a little and just give her girlfriend this smile that said there was a lot more going on than met the eye at McKinney's.

At first, they freaked me out. I mean what could two women really do in bed? I knew about dildos and stuff from all those videos that Johnny showed me but it just didn't seem like they could substitute for the real thing. Besides in the movies, a guy always showed up so that took care of wanting something other than plastic inside you. A guy always shows up in the kind of videos Johnny likes. What a surprise.

But I was worried about other stuff too. What if they decided to hit on me? How would I handle it? It wouldn't be like the guys doing it; I was used to laughing that off. I didn't even want to go into the ladies room when one of them was in there, not at first anyway. What if they went after me? They might be more persistent than the guys, might not take no for an answer. The thought got me a little hot even when it scared me most, I gotta admit.

I started watching them every chance I got, especially on slow Thursdays, just to see what they'd do. I mean I was kinda sly about it, wiping down tables, watching the TV over their heads and that kind of thing, not standing there with my mouth open like some yahoo. I didn't want to drive them off, not even when they scared me. But I started hoping that I could see them kiss, maybe watch the blonde slip her hand under the brunette's skirt and feel her up. We get plenty of that with straight couples so I figured why not with them too?

I started thinking about what the brunette's boobs would feel like in my hand, maybe with the nipples getting harder when I squeezed. I tried to imagine sucking on them, taking as much as I could into my mouth. In my head, I could see her head thrown back, her eyes closed when I did it, just like I imagined they would be with the blonde. Then I got grossed out and I stopped watching them for a while.

But my gross outs didn't last long. Soon, I started picturing them watching when I was with Johnny. Maybe they'd be naked, maybe kissing. Sometimes I pretend that Johnny was doing me while we watch them. The blonde is always going down on her girl then, sticking her hand up inside her while her tongue got busy. Johnny usually didn't want to do that so I got off imagining the brunette's face, picturing how I'd feel if it was me. But I didn't imagine one of them going down on me, not back then. That took a while.

I started thinking about what would turn them on about watching us and realized there wasn't a whole lot. We usually just did it the normal way, nothing fancy. I mean it was hot for me and all, just not as hot as I thought it could be. The night I figured that out I flipped Johnny on his back and rode his dick for a change. It angled up inside me and felt really good, especially when I kept playing with myself the whole time, rubbing myself off, making him play with my titties. We both came and damn, that was hot! And in my mind, those two were watching and getting all hot over it too. That just made it all that much better.

I didn't have the fantasy about the ladies room at first, I guess cause it freaked me out to even think about the two of them in there together, let alone being in there with me. First I started thinking about teasing them a little when I waited on their table, maybe wearing a shorter skirt or unbuttoning an extra button on my blouse. Maybe leaning across the table when I dropped off their drinks and letting them catch a peek at my tits in a nice lace bra. It wouldn't go any further than that, nossir. Just a quick look at what they wouldn't be getting when they got home.

Then one time, they went into the ladies room together. Now, I don't know for sure what they got into in there, but I'm betting it was each other. I mean they were in there longer than any business usually takes and it was a slow night so they weren't likely to be interrupted. After they left, I went in there on my break and started to think about what it would be like to hidden in one of the stalls when they were going at it. I'd be in there with my feet tucked up so they couldn't see them, just listening. They'd be in the next stall kissing and then the brunette would moan. I'd hear them whispering to each other as they pulled their shirts up.

I could just about see their breasts rubbing together. Then the blonde would lean down and take one of those big round ones in her mouth. She'd get her thigh between her girlfriend's legs and just shove against her crotch. I imagined the brunette's eyes half closed, listened to her pant in my mind until I stuck a hand between my legs. I was getting wet through my jeans. So I unbuttoned them and sat on the stool. Once I got my fingers busy, I came right away, barely had to touch my clit.

I started doing that a lot on Thursday nights if it was slow enough. If it was busy, I just worked behind the bar or worked the tables with my panties riding up between my wet lips. I really had to watch the nipples or the other customers would go nuts. So I always tried to get a "smoke break" those nights so I could take care of business.

After a couple of weeks, though, it wasn't enough to keep getting me off. Not every time any way. I needed something more for that. I mean, don't get me wrong. I love Johnny and we've been together for a couple of years now, but some times a girl needs more than that. I was glad I didn't know the blonde and her girlfriend. It would've ruined everything. Or at least made it a lot harder. This way, it was just in my head so I wasn't cheating or anything like that.

So I started upping the ante in my head during break times. First I was listening to them. Then their stall door was open and I'd be watching them. Or the brunette was up on the countertop with her legs spread and the blonde was going down on her. I'd be watching through the crack in the door, my hand between my legs. After a while, they knew I was watching and it just made it hotter. The brunette'd blow me kisses. Or she'd pull up her shirt and pinch her nipples, just to watch me squirm. It'd make her squirm too, which was almost as much fun. I was their little secret and they'd put on a show for me almost every week, with no one any the wiser.

Then I started wondering what it would be like to be in there with them whenever I got bored at work. Well, okay, I got bored at school, too. I like actuarial science and all but it gets pretty slow. So I started really building on the bathroom game. In the best version of it, the last one I had before the bar closed, I worked my way out of the stall and walked over to them when they were kissing. The brunette was up on the countertop next to the sink, her panties off and her skirt yanked up so she could wrap her legs around the blonde.

In my fantasy, it takes a minute before they realize that I'm there with them. Then the blonde turns around and kisses me instead, stepping away from the brunette to wrap her arms around me. It's a long wet kiss and her tongue feels thick and solid against mine. You can tell that she knows what she's doing. I can almost feel her hands pull up my skirt and I'm getting wetter by the second.

The brunette's standing behind me now, kissing the back of my neck while she reaches around to start unbuttoning my shirt. I can feel those long red nails brush my nipples, feel her round tits against my back. The blonde's gotten under my skirt now and I can feel her yank my panties down. I kick them away from my ankles like I've done this before, opening my eyes to watch the bathroom door. I'm almost hoping that someone walks in as the brunette gets my shirt open and the blonde leans down to run her tongue along the top of my bra. She sticks it down into my cleavage as I lean back against her friend and kiss her.

The brunette's got a whole different flavor, all smoke and perfume mixed together and now she's undoing my bra while I suck on her tongue. The blonde's got her mouth on my tit now, practically taking the whole thing in and I'm moaning even before she lets me feel her teeth on my nipple. I lean against the brunette even more and reach back to slide my hand up her skirt. Her thighs are slick and wet and I run a finger along them until I get to her crotch. Then I stick a finger inside her, just to see what it would feel like. I can feel a moan come up from inside her and she's wet and hot against my fingers. Just then the blonde switches to my other tit and her buddy pulls up my skirt.

Those long red nails that scared me so much at first are on their way up my thigh and I just wrap my free arm around the blonde's shoulders and groan. No way am I stopping this now. The brunette's fingers reach up inside me, those nails grazing my clit until I've got goosebumps all over just thinking about it.

The blonde reaches up and turns my face around as she stands up and just looks at me. No one says a word because we all know what we want. The brunette's fingers find my magic spot and start rubbing while her girlfriend sticks a hand down her own pants and starts rubbing herself off. The other hand clamps down on my boob and starts working it between her fingers, pinching my nipple until I think I'm going to fall over.

I look away, just for a minute and watch us in the mirror. The brunette's still nuzzling my neck through my hair, her eyes half closed. I can feel her pant against my skin. I'm wearing nothing but my skirt now and the blonde's still wearing all her clothes. That always turns me on even more somehow, like I'm really getting away with something. She grabs my chin and turns me back to face her. Then she kisses me again just as I come, my legs shaking so hard that they both have to hold me up. I can taste pussy juice in the blonde's mouth now, all sweet and sour rolled up together and it gets me even hotter.

I'm still shaking when they boost me up on the counter and spread my legs. They hold them open and make me watch while they kiss and the brunette sticks her hand down the other one's pants. I reach down between my own legs and the blonde reaches out and slaps my hand away. I know I'm just supposed to watch but I'm so hot and empty I can't help it.

I try again and this time the blonde turns around and sticks three fingers inside me. I hump them, groaning the whole time and playing with my own tits. I'm hoping that I'll be hot enough to distract both of them again, and 'cause it's my fantasy, I am. The blonde leans over and kisses me while she works all five fingers inside me. I spread as wide as I can, getting wetter while I watch the brunette work her hand inside her girlfriend's pants.

That's when the blonde balls her fingers up inside me and damn near punches her way to my g-spot. I close around her hand like a big glove and I howl. Then I hear the door open behind us. Sometimes I make it the manager who walks in, sometimes just any customer. I can never make up my mind if they join us while I'm thrashing around or if they just watch. Either way I put on quite a show. The blonde's way into me, driving into me until I can't see straight, leaning down to tongue my clit, then my tits and I come hard, making sounds that Johnny's never heard out of my lips.

It gets me every time, just imagining how it could have been. Sometimes I wish I had the guts to talk to them when they were still coming in on Thursday nights, other times I think it's just as well that I was too chicken shit. Once McKinney's closed, I never saw them again. I mean you can't have too many slow Thursdays and still stay open. I hear it's turned into a fern bar.

I work at an insurance company now and there's no one around like that couple, no one who I want to think about that way at least. It's not like I'm attracted to just any girl after all, just some times at lunch or when I'm taking the bus home. Then there'll be something about someone that'll remind me of them and I'll get all hot and wet thinking about it, just like on a Thursday night.

But I still got Johnny and it's gotten a little wilder between us now, especially since I started suggesting stuff. I still can't get him to do it in a bar bathroom but I'm working on it. I'm hoping it'll be even better in real life.

By the Winding Mere

When I came to myself, the ravens were at my face pecking at my eyes and the pain of the great hole in my side was near enough for me to give in. Naught but the memory of my brother's lost honor and a fear of more pain to come drove me to move both head and arm to cast them off, sending them to fly cawing to feast elsewhere on the field.

The hot blood flowed thick and fast down my side, filling my brother's armor every time I moved. I could hear the sound of human scavengers stripping the arms and valuables from my fallen host, but there was no skirl of the pipes or music of the drums to tell me that any lived beside me. The smell of death and the sweet tang of my own blood came to me with each breath. Not for this had I donned the Gray Wolf's arms and come out on the field to fight, as any good daughter of my house would have done. Now there must be none left but me. I drew a deep breath and forced myself to open my visor.

The clear gray light of the sky blinded me as I dragged myself up on my arm to survey the field. Round me the hills of bodies were piled under the circling black wings of the ravens. The Gray Wolf's standard lay where it had fallen. At first, I thought it mattered not, as the Gray Wolf was no more, but while I looked at it, I found that it still moved me. I could not leave the banner of my house to blood and rot while I yet drew breath.

The air hissed through my teeth as I dragged myself forward to seize the pole. Slowly, so slowly, I planted it in the ground before me and placed hand over hand along its length to pull myself upright. Then with my hand clutched over the hole in my armor, I shut my eyes against the destruction before me and stood swaying, the banner holding me upright.

For the first time since I awoke, I thought to call my horse and hawk. My fingers went to my lips to whistle, but found that I could make naught but the smallest sound. I slumped against the banner, thinking to sink once more to the earth, but as my hand dropped from my lips, it found my horn still at my belt.

That I brought to my mouth and blew upon it with near the last breath and hope remaining to me. The sweet blast drove the ravens from the bodies, forced the scavengers back and dropped me to my knees. If it twere not enough, I had nothing left to make another such call.

The wind sang around me, clearing away the scents of death and pain and blood for a moment and I could hear Macha's cry from far above. One of my clan had survived at least, and I smiled to think it. From below, I heard Strongheart's familiar whicker and my heart leapt. I dragged my eyes open to see my great grey steed, his flanks awash with blood, step gingerly through the corpses to reach my side. Macha flew down to land on the saddle horn with a great thump. Her unhooded eyes peered down at me. I cheered a little at their loyalty. Perhaps my brother was right when he said that I understood beasts like no other of our clan.

I began to pull myself up once again, stubbornly refusing to mourn the passing of those others that I loved. There would be time enough later, when my wounds were bound, and I was safe. The thought drew me up. If the host lay slain before me, surely Macaran's forces now held our lands. There would be no home for me to go back to.

A tear rolled down my cheek, warmed by Strongheart's breath as he pushed his nose to my shoulder. I staggered to his side, as leave the slaughter I must before a quick dagger dispatched me for my goods. But when I tried to mount, the saddle might have been a mile above me for all the chance I stood of reaching it in my armor.

The helm went first, tugged free by my trembling fingers. Next the great breastplate and greaves until soon I stood shivering in my under clothes. I tugged the long shirt up to see my wounded side and grimaced at what I saw. The lance was no longer in my side, but the wound was deep and cruel and the blood still flowed free.

I looked around me, but could see naught to bind it but Culin's love token. He lay where he had fallen, slain while protecting my back, the bloodstained scarf of his lady love still wrapped around his broad chest. I pulled it free, tears coursing now down my face. A valiant and kindly man, my brother's right hand had been, and a laughing wench had been his lady love. She would laugh no more when she heard of today's work. I planted the banner at his side, the Gray Wolf flying above him, for so he had died.

Once the scarf was bound against around my wounds and I had pulled my cloak around me, I turned once more to Strongheart. The world spun and went black as I pulled myself into the saddle. Macha flew off with a cry to land nearby as I forced myself awake.

A familiar whine pulled my eyes open. Valiant, my brother's great hound, stood on unsteady legs at Strongheart's feet. One paw he held above the ground and his jaws and muzzle were all covered in blood. I met his eyes and murmured encouragingly, and the anxious light in them died away. He had found his pack again, as I was finding mine. We would all go to find safety together or not at all. I clicked at Strongheart to start forward down the hill.

Little do I remember of that ride, with the great steed ambling surely underneath me, and poor Valiant limping behind. The wind carried on it the scent of death while it held Macha's wings as she soared behind us. On it also came the voices of the ravens, not mere caws this time, but words, words such as I could understand in my pain and fever, though I knew not how. They told an old tale of a witch living far to the west, one who lived on the edges of a great mere. It was said that she and she alone could heal the wounds of battle and the pain of war. With no more than this, I turned Strongheart's head to the west, for home lay behind me and there was no going back.

We journeyed some days, moving far from the battlefield and the lands I knew. With each dawning, I knew I had to find the witch soon, for my wound stopped bleeding yet did not close. I bound Valiant's paw so that he limped less and cleaned both our wounds, but I could do no more. Macha hunted for all three of us, laying the hares and small birds before me to skin and to cook while Strongheart found his own feed.

At night I lay wrapped in my cloak and dreamed of a woman. Her hair was black as night, and shone like silver shot through with ebony. Her eyes were green, like emeralds, like cats, and sometimes like the leaves in the forest, so changed they with her mood. Her face was beautiful when she was human, but sometimes in my dreams it changed like her eyes, and then she was part woman, part great cat or horse or fish. Time and again, I tried to cry out, "Help me!" But it seemed she heard me not.

Some nights I dreamed of the gentle touch of hands upon my body, the sweet kiss of tender lips, the soft touch of a tongue upon my breast. Those nights, my body burned as if on fire, and I longed to see the witch with the eyes of love, for I thought it must be her though I could not see her face.

Hands stroked between my legs in those dreams, driving hard and then soft within me, withdrawing and driving in once more. I could feel the fingers clench inside me, feel myself wet with a desire I had never known before. The mouth upon my breast grew hotter, scalding my flesh as it slipped lower on my body. Soon I felt a tongue slide between my legs and inside me, tasting me and stroking upward, sending flames burning along my legs until I shook with ecstasy.

My wound pained me less when I awoke from such dreams, but my spirit ached still from my losses. My brother, our friends, our home, all gone. Even such dreams as these could not drive the pain of defeat from me. Anger burned through me and pushed me onward. Macaran would pay. So we wandered on, roaming westward, ever westward, in hopes of hearing some word of the witch who could help me win my vengeance.

The day came when Macha brought a live hare, wounded but still moving to lay at my feet as we rested by a little brook. I caught the beast to give it the final blow and its eyes captured mine. They were yellow against the gleam of its soft gray fur and I could feel its thoughts as though they were my own. *Spare me* it seemed to say *and I will tell you where you need to search.* Perhaps I was bespelled. I knew not. I met the Valiant's hungry eyes and Macha's cold dark gaze above the hare's head, then looked once more at the beast.

Again I heard the plea and a picture came to me, an image of a great high mountain to the west, lit by moonlight. A great owl sat in a high pine, its golden eyes peering wisely down at us as we journeyed to the foot of the tree. *Seek the owl*, the hare seemed to say. *What you seek lies not far beyond.* As if I dreamed, I set the creature down and ordered Macha and Valiant back. It limped into the bushes and disappeared, leaving my beasts to watch me as though I ran mad. Macha leapt into the air with a cry. I hoped then she went for other prey, for I had no strength for hunting, and I fell asleep before she returned.

When I awoke with the lark's song in the morning, I could see the mountain before us, where I had seen nothing in the dusk of the night before. There we must go and so we went, Valiant now with scarcely a limp, and Macha first flying before us, then riding on my shoulder. I could sit a little straighter in the saddle this morn, and the wound had closed a bit. Some magic was surely at work here, for though it would not heal, yet it did not fester. I thought of gentle hands in the night and I smiled, swaying in the saddle as I relied on Strongheart to take me the smoothest way as we traveled.

His feet were sure as he bore me along to the foot of the great mountain, and carefully he took me around the low branches that might have knocked me off. The mountain was steep, with huge bald cliffs and moss-covered boulders standing against the trunks of the tall pines and the cold gray sky of the twilight. Higher and higher we went until I could see all the surrounding country, and before me stood the tallest tree in all the woods that grew on that long slope. The wind sang through its branches as though it were the giant harp of our hold. It sang songs of valor, of courage and of the peace to come. I shivered, for were those not the very songs that drove me to the field in the Gray Wolf's armor?

I looked up. As the hare had said, the snow white owl sat looking down at me and I felt it knew my heart. Strongheart stopped at the foot of the tree, and Valiant and Macha sat waiting for me to do what

I would. The ancient golden eyes held mine as I looked up, and I thought hard on my wound and on what had gone before, the image of the black-haired woman overlaid against it all. A long moment passed and I clasped my hands together, as though entreating the bird, as indeed I was.

A thought came to me then of a mere on the other side of the mountain. I saw myself walking to its edge with a bundle of flowers in my hand: goldenrod, St. John's Wort, and other herbs that held magic within them. Strongheart, Macha and Valiant were not to be seen, but my horn was yet at my side.

In my vision, I threw the herbs into the water and drew back at what I saw. Then I drew a blast on my horn and found myself again at the foot of the tree, gazing upward. I knew not what I saw in the lake, for in my vision, I could only see myself. Yet it was clear to me that I must ride on, then dismount and walk before I reached the mere. I saluted the owl and turned Strongheart's head down the mountain, and the wind played songs of a journey's end on the great tree as we rode away.

I dreamed that night of the Gray Wolf. My brother came to meet me with the wounds that had killed him still unhealed and looked at me with the eyes of the dead. "You fought well, my sister but still we lost all. Macaran's hands run red with our blood and we know no rest in our homelands." I could see Culin standing by his right hand, as he had in life, and the rest of our slaughtered host gathered behind him. "Give us peace, little sister. Set us free."

There could be no doubt as to how I was to do this. Once I was healed, I should have to go and hunt for Macaran, for only vengeance could set my brother and our followers free. So I had been taught since I was but a cub.

I shivered as I lay awake, soaked in a cold sweat and staring upward at the white, round moon. Macaran was a strong leader of men, a greater warrior than I, and probably stronger even than the Wolf. How I was to defeat him, I knew not, but do it I must for I could not face the eyes of the sorrowful dead each night as I slept. The light of madness fired my brain at the thought, until I pushed it away, falling at last into a troubled sleep.

I rode onward the next day and the day after until we came to a
large green meadow, dotted with small pale blue flowers. The mere
was in sight in the distance, and I slid from Strongheart's back, trying
not to wince as I landed. I wanted to take the saddle from his back,
but feared that I could not remount without its aid. I slipped the bridle
from his ears instead, and hung it from the pommel. My voice shook
as I ordered them all to stay and gave them a final pat. Valiant's head
cocked to one side, puzzled eyes following me as I left, but he obeyed.
I told myself that he would bring the others when I needed them, and
walked on with a quavering heart.

The edge of the meadow led through a small wood, then into a
field of tall grasses that marked the edge of the mere. I found the herbs
that I needed along the way, and walked, slowly and painfully to the
edge of the water. Holding the blossoms to my breast, I offered a hope
for my healing and threw them into the water.

The water boiled before me and the fish sprang into the air, their
flight curving and their scales gleaming in the pale sunlight as they
flew upward, then down, down far below the surface. The water birds
flew squawking from the water's surface as the center of the mere
became a whirlpool. The water spun round and round and my heart
nearly misgave me. Why would she heal me when I had so disturbed
her?

The waters parted and she came forth, part of her a woman, the
rest a fish, just as I had dreamt. She leapt upward and turning, saw
me. An angry blaze glowed in her eyes and I clapped my horn to my
lips and blew, my hands shaking. Her head drew back and she looked
behind me. I could hear Macha's call and Valiant's belling tones on the
wind. The witch sprang from the waters, half of her now a great mare,
and she galloped over the water to the mere's edge. The earth shook
behind me as Strongheart charged to my side, and I dragged myself
into the saddle once more. I held on as I urged my steed to follow.
"Catch her!" I ordered Macha and Valiant, little thinking how this was
to be done, for I cared for nothing but the healing of my wounds by
then.

We coursed along behind her, and Valiant ran until his sides
heaved, yet we drew no closer. I could see Macha buffeted by the

winds above and I began to lose hope. Fleet of foot was the witch in her mare's form, and hard though Strongheart's hooves pounded upon the earth as he followed her, he drew no closer.

The gallop jarred through my wound, and the pain washed through my head until I reeled in the saddle, the field a sea of red around me. I held on until despair filled me, and my hands slipped from the saddle, for if we could not catch her, I would surely die. What was there to hold on for? My brother's face, his eyes filled with the cold anguish of the restless dead, danced before me as I dropped like a stone from Strongheart's back. Then, all was darkness.

I do not in truth know what happened next. In my fever dream, I thought I saw the witch standing before me in her maiden's form, Macha sitting quiescent on her ungloved hand. "Do you know nothing but the ways of war?" Her angry voice rang round my head, and I remembered nothing more.

When I came back to myself, some time later, I lay naked, not in a field by the mere, but instead in a small wooden bed by a fireside. The firelight flickered on the beams above me, and I could see the dawn outside the small window.

She sat beside me in a dark blue velvet gown, with her long black hair unbound and shining about her shoulders. The green eyes watched me from a face as beautiful as I had seen in my dreams. In the mirror behind her I could see myself as she saw me, my brown hair cut short to fit beneath a helm, my long nose broken from a fall during arms practice.

But it was my deeds that made her look at me in anger and I hung my head as best I could against the high down pillows. It seemed as though all that I had done ill, whether in battle, or at home, was weighed in the balance against my heart. I remembered when I followed my brother to lay waste to the lands of Macaran, from the crops we burned to the men I slew to plant the banner of the Gray Wolf farther afield than in our father's time. In truth, I had been a warrior like my father and my brother before me. I knew no other way until now. For the first time, I questioned the way of the sword.

"I know that you seek healing at my hands, and without it, you will die. My creed compels me to save you," she said softly. "Know this. I can lie a night with you and make you hale and sound as before. No lance or sword or any weapon made of iron can touch you when you rise. Yet you may not raise iron against another. No harm can you do in battle. Think well upon this, warrior, and choose what will be." With that, she stood and left me to my thoughts.

Long I pondered her words. My wound might close on its own in time, or it might fester. The pain of my side and my spirit lay balanced against what I owed to my brother and to our people. The banner of the Gray Wolf rode before my eyes until I forced it aside to see what lay beneath. Macaran's host laid waste to our lands as we had laid waste to his, and so it went, back through the generations.

It was said that my great-grandmere married a Macaran to bring an end to it all, as it had for a time. But ever the expanding border called and the good grazing lands of the Macaran Clan called us down from our mountains and our mines. The iron was less each year, and the sheep and the kine grew lean, and honor decreed that we fight. Better by far for the House of the Gray Wolf to fall to the sword rather than to starve. And fall we had, until I alone remained. It was too much. There must be a better way.

I lay on that bed until she came back to me. This time, I raised my hand to hers and clasped it in mine. I said nothing, but met her eyes as I pulled her down beside me for a kiss and pushed the blankets aside. Soft her lips were against mine, as they were in my dream, and her tongue slid gently into my mouth, as I parted my legs to her questing thigh and hand. I opened my heart as well and yielded it up to her as her lips caressed my neck, passing slowly to my breast. She took it in her mouth and pulled upon it, her teeth grazing my flesh, her tongue drawing up a river of fire.

How came the goldenrod to her hand I knew not but she stroked my wound with its flowers, drawing the swelling down. Once, twice, three times, she ran her tongue round its edges and the fire burned within me. Some words she sang, and the sound of them stung my skin, until I could feel no pain from my wound.

Her fingers ran slowly up between my legs and the flames followed them, as they passed inside me as she had done in my dreams before.

I burned and opened wide before her, and her fingers found my secret places and caressed and thrust against them. Her thigh drove her hand deep within me until I could feel its length inside me and I welcomed it. I closed around it, as she withdrew and returned again. Now her tongue slipped between my legs as well, lapping gently and firmly against me until my back arched, and the fire rode my body until I shook with its force.

I opened my eyes as the flames died away to see my wound closing slowly, flesh drawn to flesh as though it had a mind of its own. The witch sat up so that she was stretched across my body and I could slip my fingers inside her. Wet she was, and soft against my questing hand. Her juices poured out like molten gold over my fingers and across my wound. The sting was nothing as I took her breast in my other hand. The fire filled her as it had filled me and she moaned, the sound shaking us both to our cores.

My breath quickened and I pushed my hand further into her. The long black hair trailed against my legs as she bent her head back, pushing her breast further into my hand. I rolled it between my fingers, running my other hand in and out of her as I did so. Her body shook and she gave a great cry, collapsing on her hands over me, the long hair making a black tent that covered us both.

I pulled her down beside me, my lips finding hers and her breath hot and sweet against my mouth. Her flesh loosened against me until she felt soft again and I slipped my hand between her legs once more. She gasped and I pulled her on top of me so that I still lay on my back, but my mouth was between her legs.

My tongue drank in her taste of wild honey and I breathed deep the musky scent of foxes and warm earth. Slowly I caressed her finding all of her secret places and tasting them, coaxing them. She arched her back once more, hands placed behind her as she pushed against my mouth. The fire rode us both, sharp, hot flames that burned, but did no harm, dancing along her legs until we shook as one and our cries filled the room.

She lay with me the whole of that night and by morning, we knew each other's bodies well. When I awoke with the dawn, I could see that my wound was but a scar. No Gray Wolf's banner danced before me in her bed, and my spirit was lighter. I still knew not what I would do, but I knew that I was not as I had been before. Her eyes opened slowly and met mine and we kissed. I thought to ask if I might stay, but I knew the answer before she spoke.

"I cannot lie with the wolf's cub each night," she said gently, fingers stroking my ribs. "You must see what you are become."

"May I return when I know?"

"I will not refuse you."

That gave me hope as her lips caressed mine once more and she moved swiftly from the room. No more of her did I see that day, but food for my morning meal and food for my journey she left me. Strongheart I found in a field outside, Macha on the rooftop and Valiant at the door. My sword I buried in the field. I did not look back as my horse and my hawk and my brindled hound and I rode forth to see what lay ahead for one who would leave the Wolf's path.

An Evening in Estelí

Lorraine watched the other woman as if nothing else mattered. For a moment, it wasn't 1988 and they weren't at a Sandinista rally in Estelí, surrounded by swaying Nicaraguans singing "No Pasaran!" For once teaching people to read was the furthest thing from her mind.

It was as if they were the only two people in the world. The feeling made her heart race, tumbling over inside her until she thought she'd pass out. She imagined kissing the other woman, feeling her lips open beneath her own. She pictured the softness of the woman's breasts in her currently empty hands and the image sent a wave of pure desire through her.

But then the crowd cheered and the noise broke into her reverie. With a huge effort, she turned to speak to another member of her brigade, mumbling something inane about how hot it was. Derek gave her a blank stare, then nodded in agreement, his mind somewhere else.

For a minute, she thought about asking him if he knew who the mysterious beauty was but then decided against it. Derek had excellent subliminal gaydar, judging from his last two girlfriends. He'd introduce himself to the gorgeous stranger, they'd date and she'd come out eventually. Then she'd come and cry on Lorraine's shoulder before going off to date someone else. It had happened twice now and there was no way she was going through it again. Lorraine resigned herself to surreptitious glances.

The woman could have been Nicaraguan but Lorraine didn't think so. Too tall, for one thing. She had golden brown skin, big brown eyes and glorious long black hair that flowed down her back in a ponytail. Her hands were big for her size and her body was compact but well-rounded. Right now, she was talking to some of the market women, making them laugh.

She had the most kissable mouth Lorraine had ever seen: full lips that parted in a big smile to show slightly crooked white teeth, gapped in the middle. Lorraine wanted to run her tongue up that gap and behind those teeth. The notion send a red-hot flash through her, leaving an empty pang in its wake. She made herself look away. Maybe there was something to be said for unfulfilled crushes after all.

It wasn't like she was liable to see much in the way of fulfillment anyway, even if the other woman did turn out to be a lesbian. For one thing, it wasn't safe. For another, there was nowhere to go; she slept in the guesthouse in hammocks with the rest of her brigade. None of them ever went anywhere by themselves if they could help it. You never knew when the contras might strike; Nicaragua was a country at war and forgetting that was a bad, potentially fatal, idea.

The commander on the makeshift stage yielded his place to Daisy Zamora, poet and soldier. Lorraine reminded herself that this was the reason she'd come down here: to help build a revolution of poets, not to find herself a new girlfriend. Of course, it was turning out to be more complicated than that but she still kept her ideals close to her heart. Listening to the poet, she almost forgot the gorgeous woman in the flow of equally gorgeous words.

When Zamora finished, Lorraine broke into cheers along with the rest of the crowd. Everything after this would be one big party until everybody had to crawl off to bed before another day in the coffee fields, the clinics and the schools. Or the battlefields in the mountains. Lorraine grimaced sympathetically at the young Sandinista solders walking back to their barracks for nightly guard duty.

"I like her work even more than Ernesto's. So much raw energy. Have you read Giaconda's poems? They're a bit like that too." The voice at her side was a deep contralto, English edged with a slight accent that Lorraine didn't recognize. She turned, heart thumping, to find the beauty standing a mere yard away. She was, of course, talking to Derek. Lorraine forced herself not to roll her eyes or groan out loud. Damn the man, how did he manage to do this time and again?

Disgusted, she turned on her heel to walk back to the guesthouse. "Wait, Lorrie, there's someone you should meet," Derek's voice pulled her back, reminded her to appear gracious however little she felt it. "This is Marla. She's here working on a series of articles on women in the Revolution. Lorraine's been on the brigade with me for four months now." He grinned as if he could somehow take the credit for Lorraine's being there in the first place.

But Marla didn't seem to notice. Instead, she reached over and caught Lorraine's hand in one of her larger ones. Her touch sent a shock through Lorraine that only intensified when she met the other woman's eyes. Gradually she realized that Marla had asked her a question and she hadn't heard a word of it. A blush burned through her cheeks and she made herself look away for an instant. "I'm sorry, I spaced out. What did you say?"

Marla's full lips quirked in an amused smile. "Daisy's poetry has that effect on me sometimes too. I asked where in the States you were from and how long you'll be in Nicaragua."

Of course she had. What did you expect her to ask? Lorraine managed a small smile and answered, "I'm from New York City. Brooklyn. I'll be here for another six weeks, then I have to go back to my job. You?"

A wave of singing Nicaraguans swept by just then, swirling down the street like a river as they headed for a nearby square. One of the men caught Derek's arm and towed him along, leaving Marla and Lorraine to trail after them. They sang along for a few minutes until they came to one of Lorraine's favorite murals and she stopped to admire it.

It was a simple harvest scene, just a group of women picking coffee beans, painted on a house wall on a narrow street. If you turned right, you could see the mountains, left and you could see the rest of the town. Lorraine loved the view almost as much as the faces of the painted women, which seemed alight with hope and enthusiasm.

Marla stopped with her and was quiet while they studied the painting. Finally she cleared her throat and said softly, "This is a lovely one. I don't think I've ever stopped to look at it before. Thank you."

Lorraine looked at her and grinned. "I love this mural. It's like the painted version of why I came here to try and help." She stopped, feeling embarrassed and changed the subject. "So you never did say where you were from."

Marla's eyes were still fixed on the painting. "I think I know what you mean. I love their faces. Marvelous." She was quiet for a moment before she continued, "From? Oh everywhere, I suppose. The States and Spain for the majority of my life but I have lived in many other countries. As for how long I stay, well that depends on how long the article takes me. That and one or two other things." Marla flashed her a blinding grin.

The breath caught in Lorraine's throat for a moment or a lifetime. She wasn't quite sure which but she hoped she wasn't being as obvious as she was afraid she was. She made herself smile back, ask if Marla wanted to go to one of the little cafes on the next plaza. Anything to prevent her from disappearing too soon. Marla must have accepted but Lorraine didn't hear a word until they started walking.

The little voice of her common sense told her that now was the time to let Marla know that she wasn't all culture-shocked or just plain nuts. It got some of the foreigners that way, between the poverty and the war. They just got overwhelmed and ended up acting weird then leaving early, long before their volunteer time was up. But she wasn't like that. At least she hadn't thought so until today. She made her lips form words, "What magazine are you writing for? Do you do a lot of journalism?"

Marla glanced at her sidelong, dark eyes half-lidded in a way that Lorraine found unbearably sexy. That, of course, was when Derek called to them from a cafe they were passing, cutting off whatever Marla had been about to say. Lorraine cursed silently as they walked over to join him. He was sitting with a few of the other brigade leaders and they were in the midst of an intense conversation about the best techniques for teaching literacy.

But at least Marla was sitting next to her. That was something. She made herself ask questions, throw in a few things she had read. Truly, she loved teaching people to read and write, but somehow today, she wanted something more. The feeling grew and grew until she couldn't resist it. On impulse, she turned to Marla and whispered, "Come walk with me."

Marla gave her a startled look and Lorraine could see her consider whether or not she wanted anything to do with this strange American. The moment stretched and Lorraine regretted having said it, regretted having said anything at all. Then, like an unexpected sunrise, Marla smiled, kissable lips beckoning until Lorraine thought she might kiss her then and there. But then Marla nodded and they made their excuses to the others and the moment receded, leaving only the memory of desire in its place.

Marla talked about her article and her research as they walked and Lorraine floated on the sound of her voice, letting it thrum through her bones. Once Marla came too close and brushed her arm. Her touch sent a white-hot flash through Lorraine's entire body and her knees shook, almost dropping her to the dirt. They stopped at the top of one of the hilly streets in a nearly deserted plaza and Marla gestured to the starry sky and the mountains around them, "We are fortunate to be here, don't you think? So much beauty."

Lorraine murmured, "And pain. It's not like we can forget that part. I think being here has changed me forever." She looked out at the mountains and closed her lips on the thought that had nearly followed: *And being with you might change me even more.* After all, that was crazy; she'd just met this woman.

Marla gave her a long intent look. Lorraine could almost feel her stare burn away a patch of her hair before she turned and met the other woman's eyes. It was like a lightening strike, burning away all of Lorraine's fears in an instant. She reached out and grasped the back of Marla's neck then pulled her close for a kiss.

Those lips she'd been longing for were hard under her own at first and she could feel Marla begin to stiffen and pull away. She knew she should let go but instead she let some of her desperate longing flow into her own lips, letting them soften and open. Marla hesitated a moment longer, then slipped her arms around Lorraine's waist. The curves of their bodies meshed together and Lorraine could feel their hearts race like they were one big creature. Her breath caught in her mouth until she thought she might never breathe again.

Then Marla's lips opened under hers and she slipped her tongue inside Lorraine's mouth. She tasted sweet, like mangoes and horchata, and something about it tore a tiny moan from Lorraine's throat. That seemed to be what Marla needed to hear and her arms tightened.

It was almost enough to make them both forget where they were. But then there was the sound of market carts, of drunken singing from somewhere nearby, and Lorraine could feel her fears return. This wasn't safe, not here, not now. It took everything she had to break off the kiss. "We can't stay here." She looked into Marla's eyes, now gone so dark they were nothing but pupil.

"What's the matter, *gringa*? You want to get us all hot and bothered then chicken out?" Marla's voice was joking as she leaned in to run her tongue down Lorraine's neck. "I'm staying with friends too so I think it's here or nowhere." She pulled away for a moment, looking around them, then pulled at Lorraine's resisting hand. "Come on, little one. I know you want to." She grinned again, her eyes glittering with excitement.

Lorraine hesitated a moment longer. If the drunken men found them or if the Contras attacked, a moment of ecstasy out here, far from safety, could be deadly. But…it had been so long and she was so very wet, so very empty. She closed her eyes for a moment, imagining the feel of Marla's fingers inside her. Before she knew it, her feet moved of their own accord, following Marla toward whatever place she thought would be safe enough for the moment.

They followed a winding street away from the plaza and into the darkness, lit only by a sliver of moon. Lorraine stumbled over some trash but Marla pulled her upright and kept walking. Around a corner, she pressed Lorraine against a dried mud wall and kissed her, their mouths merging urgent and wet.

Marla pulled away to reach down and tug Lorraine's shirt up. With a gesture that suggested some practice, she pulled Lorraine's breast free of her bra and leaned down to take her already hardened nipple into her mouth. Marla tongued the hardened nub of Lorraine's flesh against her front teeth until she got a strangled yelping moan in response. Then she twisted so that she could drive her thigh between Lorraine's legs. She shoved her leg upward, rocking against the aching wetness between Lorraine's legs until Lorraine buried her fingers in her hair and rode her thigh.

At first Lorraine tried to look around, tried to remain watchful even though Marla's touch demanded a response. But it had been months, nearly a year since she'd been with anyone. Besides, it felt so good to give in, to feel so good while her heart raced at the thought of the danger. She felt more alive than she had in ages.

Marla unzipped her jeans and switched her mouth to Lorraine's other breast. Lorraine gasped as Marla's hard fingers drove their way into her pants, then up inside her. Suddenly her emptiness was more than filled and she tried her best to stretch wider to get them all in. Marla's thumb found her clit as Marla rocked forward again, using her thigh to force her fingers even deeper inside Lorraine.

Lorraine bit her lip hard to keep from yelling and moaning as loud as she could. She heard a sound off to their left and forced her eyes open wide enough to see something scuttle away in the darkness. Marla must've sensed her distraction because she nipped her breast, just hard enough to pull Lorraine away from thinking about anything around her. She rode Marla's fingers until the sensation overwhelmed her and she came, shivering and shaking, her moans muffled by Marla's mouth.

Still, she made enough noise to draw attention. There was a burst of song nearby, followed by a shout. Marla dragged Lorraine's shirt down and tugged her hand out her jeans. She shook Lorraine a little to hurry her, as if she wasn't already fumbling with the zipper on her jeans. Still wrestling with it, she trailed after Marla as they walked quickly down the alley heading for the more populated squares further down the mountain.

The man lurched out of the shadows and caught her arm before she had time to run or react. For a moment, she froze and he wrapped his arms around her, crooning endearments in Spanish in her ear. She shuddered and tried to pull away but he was stronger.

Suddenly Marla was there, her Spanish staccato and commanding. Lorraine held her breath as she demanded to know what this man intended with her sister. Marla named one of the Sandinista commanders, threatening retaliation if anything happened to them. Lorraine shuddered, waiting for the moment that the man's arms relaxed.

Instead he yelled at Marla, the noise bringing his friends. She could hear the sound of more men headed their way. She twisted away in a half-forgotten move from a long ago self-defense class, and slammed her elbow into him. Then she drove her hand upward under his chin, knocking him backward. She grabbed Marla's hand and they ran for it, drunken shouts trailing after them.

They zigzagged through alleyways and streets for what seemed like forever but couldn't have been more than fifteen minutes. Finally, they stumbled out into the square that they'd left earlier. Derek and a few of the other volunteers were still sitting at the same table, the remains of their dinner in front of them. He waved to them and Lorraine could see his eyes drop to where her hand still clutched Marla's. For a moment, she almost dropped it, nearly let go like their fingers were on fire.

But Marla's hand held firmly onto hers and she resisted the urge. Derek smiled and moved his chair over to make room for them. They sat down and ordered dinner. Lorraine excused herself to go to the restaurant's tiny outhouse and tuck herself all the way back into her clothes. She stopped in the doorway on her way back in and watched Marla for a minute before she walked out. Her legs were still shaky but she wanted nothing more than to watch the other woman talk and laugh, at least for a moment.

She had to wonder if Marla had done this before, had so many near misses and half-finished seductions that this one was commonplace. Marla glanced up then, catching her eyes. Those beautiful, kissable lips curved in a smile that was just for her and Lorraine melted, smiling back until it seemed like her face would split.

She came back to the table and ate, only just managing not to look at Marla the whole time. After that, they walked Marla back to her friend's house, and Lorraine went, slowly and reluctantly, back to the guesthouse with Derek. Marla had some interviews to do in some of the surrounding towns and was leaving at dawn. She promised she'd be back in two or three days, giving Lorraine a look that promised lovely, passionate things alongside some measure of reassurance.

Lorraine bit her lips, barely restraining herself from following Marla inside. She wanted to drop to her knees in the house's little courtyard, desperate with longing to bury her face between Marla's legs. She imagined the way she would taste, sweet and sour mixed with mango and she bit her lip in frustration. She had three interminable days before her to do nothing to do but work and fall in love with a stranger.

As the days passed, she imagined a life spent working with Marla on her articles. They would do important, prize-winning work that would change the world around them for the better. She imagined books on women in El Salvador, in Columbia, imagined traveling all over Central and South America, documenting abuses and triumphs.

She knew it was crazy to feel this way about someone she barely knew, at least when she was wide-awake and working. But at night, her hand slipped between her legs as she lay in her hammock and she pictured Marla's tongue, Marla's fingers in place of her own. She came very quietly, longing leaving a dull ache in place of the barely satisfied desire she hoped for.

By the third day, she was feverishly impatient and at first the time crawled by. It was her volunteer day at the clinic and she spent the morning washing cloths for bandages, checking the sparse inventory of medicines and cleaning. Once the doctor asked for her help with a patient who'd been shot, and she stood at his side handing him antibiotics and bandages as he needed them. She even held the wounded man's hand while the doctor dug the bullet out, wincing as his grip tightened to the almost unbearable, then gradually loosened.

It was enough to drive Marla from her mind for the moment, reminding her that she was here to help in whatever way she could. There were more patients after that, each one in need, and she was exhausted by the time she left. Part of her still hoped that Marla would be back today but now she remembered how long it could take to travel from town to town on mined roads in the back of a pickup truck. She imagined Marla wounded in an ambush or worse, the thought making her hurt more than she had thought possible after four months here.

She ate with her brigade, her mind spinning horrible visions until she wanted to go out into the countryside looking for Marla. But that was impossible so she tried to learn to wait. Finally, she went for a walk and stopped to look at her mural. It helped a little, giving her hope when it seemed like there might not be any.

That was where Marla found her, just as Lorraine had hoped she would. She caught the other woman up in a fierce hug, whispering urgently about how glad she was to see her again, to see her safe. She lit up when she saw Marla's tired smile and all the longings that she'd been trying to hold at bay flooded back through her.

They sat at a café and talked, drinking bitter coffee and juice for hours without touching. This time they talked about the things they'd seen and done and who they were before they'd come to this little war-torn country. But they didn't talk about hopes for the future or how they felt about each other. Each time Lorraine tried to find the words, they were too fearful to emerge. It seemed too shallow, too soon to speak of love, so instead they talked of other things.

Still, it made Lorraine's other fears seem less important. When the café closed, Marla came back to the brigade's guesthouse with Lorraine. They spent the night in Lorraine's hammock wrapped in each other arms, their dreams full of each other. When the rest of the brigade woke in the morning, no one said anything beyond the usual. There were a few surprised glances but that was it. Lorraine's fears seemed groundless and she nearly forgot about their first night together, how close they had been to danger. Marla kissed her when she left to go to work and the touch of her lips seemed to glow on Lorraine's own for hours.

That night, they pooled some of their scarce Nicaraguan cash and rented a room in a guesthouse that a friend of Marla's had told her about. Now Lorraine found herself wondering whether it would be like it was in the plaza. Were all her newfound feelings born from the thrill of doing something dangerous? She was almost reluctant as she trailed Marla into their room. They stood and watched each other for a moment, neither sure of what to do next.

Then Marla stepped forward and wrapped her arms around her and those kissable lips met hers. Her lips opened under the pressure, her tongue finding the gap in Marla's teeth. She caressed it slowly, savoring the taste of Marla's mouth, reveling in the small shudder that went through the other woman's body. Marla's hands were sliding the way around her, caressing her body all the way down to her ass and pulling her close. Her breath was coming in little gasps already as she maneuvered one of her own hands under Marla's shirt, stroking the silky skin over her ribs.

She worked her way up to cup one of Marla's full breasts, her thumb stroking her already erect nipple into nearly unbearable sensitivity. She pulled away from Marla's lips and let her tongue trail down her neck to her collarbone, smiling when she heard the breath catch in Marla's throat. She shivered Marla slipped one of her hands down inside her pants and began to rub her fingers along as much of Lorraine's wet slit as she could reach. Marla circled the edge of her asshole, not quite probing inside but close enough that every one of Lorraine's nerve endings felt like it was on fire.

She squirmed away a little, not wanted to break away from Marla's touch, but wanting the moment to last as long as possible. She twisted around so she could take Marla's breast in her mouth, sucking on her nipple until she could feel Marla shiver and shake from the pressure. She unzipped her jeans then, pushing her hand down into Marla's bush and the soft, aching wetness beyond it. Marla moaned softly and shifted her own hand around so that she could reach inside Lorraine.

Lorraine stroked her way inside Marla, her fingers slick and wet with the other woman's juices. Then she stepped back and tugged off first her own shirt, then Marla's. Their bras followed, then their pants, tugged free with an urgency that Lorraine had never felt before. She wanted to feel the length of Marla's naked body pressed against her own, feel the silky moist texture of her skin beneath her fingers and tongue.

Marla laughed, her chin tilted back and her throat exposed in a moment of unguarded joy. She pulled Lorraine down onto the bed next to her and kissed her hard, her tongue filling Lorrie's mouth as it explored. Lorraine worked her thigh between Marla's, mimicking Marla's move of a few nights before and using the pressure of her leg to work her fingers up inside the other woman.

Marla's moan was deep and long, vibrating down until it seemed like it shook Lorraine's fingers. Lorraine found Marla's clit, slick with want and rubbed hard, her touch fierce as Marla rolled onto her back, legs tense then body shaking with release. Her hips bucked against Lorraine's fingers and she wailed softly into Lorraine's neck.

Lorraine pulled herself up on top of Marla, fingers never relinquishing their pressure on her clit. Then she trailed her face over Marla's sweat-soaked skin, licking the salty-tang from it until she could bury her face between Marla's legs. There she manipulated Marla's clit with her tongue, trying to make it convey all of her fears and longings of the last few days. She swiped it over Marla's wet slit, once, twice, then returned to sucking on her clit as hard as she could.

Marla's hips bucked against her and the moan that came from her now was long and low, like a wild animal's. It shook Lorraine at the same time that it aroused her beyond any lovemaking she'd ever known. She tried to burrow closer, tried to lose herself in Marla's body but the journalist dragged her face away, pulling her up for a kiss. "Too much right now," she gasped before her lips met Lorraine's.

They kissed slowly and quietly for a long moment. Then Marla pulled away, stroking Lorraine's damp hair from her cheek. "I have to go to Managua the day after tomorrow. Come with me." She could see something in Lorraine's face before she spoke and she pressed one finger to Lorraine's lips. "No, don't tell me now. Tell me in the morning." She smiled and for that instant, Lorraine was all hers.

Lorraine pressed her lips to Marla's finger, then pulled it into her mouth. Slowly and carefully, she sucked on each of her fingers, her tongue swiping against Marla's palm until Marla growled. She caught Lorraine by the shoulders and flipped them both over so that she lay on top of Lorraine this time. Her fingers were hard and undeniable as she drove them inside Lorraine, stretching her like she had in the alley a few nights before.

Lorraine was ready for her this time though and the pressure felt good, no, more than good as she rode Marla's fingers to release. Her hips bucked and heaved and she murmured endearments in Spanish and English as she came. They lay wrapped in each other arms for the rest of the night, waking periodically to kiss and caress each other.

But the next morning, she still didn't have an answer to Marla's request. She knew she wanted the journalist desperately but she had responsibilities here. Besides, what if she was wrong? She couldn't bring herself to tell Marla, not yet. Instead, she slipped out quietly while Marla was still asleep. She bought a roll and drank some coffee at a little stand while she thought. Then she went for a walk, her feet taking her back to the mural before she even realized it was happening.

She stood there looking at it, thinking about why she'd come here. She thought first about what she thought she could do, then she thought about what she liked about the mural. A few moments later, she began walking back to the guesthouse, her decision made. If she had known it, her face looked a bit like that of the women in the painting, looking toward the future with hope despite the risks.

Acknowledgements

Many thanks to Steve, whose idea this book was and without whom it would not exist, and to Jana, who patiently read and commented on the manuscript in progress, not to mention putting up with the author. Thanks also to Lorraine Inzalaco for generously providing her lovely artwork for the cover (signed and numbered prints are available from the artist from www.inzalaco-lesbianart. com).

Thanks also to the various editors who selected some of these stories for previous anthologies and last but certainly not least, to my friends and colleagues for their encouragement.

About the Author

Catherine Lundoff has done a lot of stuff. For the last decade or so she has lived in Minneapolis with her talented and very cool girlfriend and a cat or two. She writes fiction and nonfiction, holds down a day job as an IT contractor and occasionally does other things in her copious free time. Prior to moving to Minneapolis, she held down a motley collection of careers which included: professional archaeologist, law student, scorer of standardized tests, d.j., research assistant and part-time receptionist.

She dreams of spending her days lolling about on a daybed eating bonbons and being terribly witty. Or possibly sailing the *Spanish Main*, cutlass in hand.

She is the author of an ebook collection of lesbian erotica, *Night's Kiss* (Torquere Press, 2005) and her numerous short stories and articles have appeared in some of the more acclaimed and noted anthologies of erotic fiction.

Printed in the United States
108537LV00002B/297/A